Nina Berberova

THREE NOVELS
The Second Volume

❦

The Cloak
The Black Pestilence
The Comb

Translated from the Russian by
Marian Schwartz

Chatto & Windus
LONDON

Published in 1991 by
Chatto & Windus Ltd
20 Vauxhall Bridge Road
London SW1V 2SA

A CIP catalogue record is available
for this book from the British Library

ISBN 0 7011 3632 4

Copyright © Actes Sud 1990, 1989, 1991
Translation copyright © Marian Schwartz 1991

Typeset by The Spartan Press Ltd
Lymington, Hants

Printed and bound in Great Britain by
Butler & Tanner Ltd, Frome, Somerset

CONTENTS

The Cloak   1

The Black Pestilence   69

The Comb   153

The Cloak

The Cloak

I

My sister's name was Ariadna. I was nine that unforgettable, snowy, hungry winter when she finished school and became a grown-up. That was the year my mother died too, in one of Petersburg's cold, desolate clinics. In the space of two months our whole life changed, and so did we.

There had been a modest but comfortable apartment, a maid who never let me out of the door without inspecting me first, my eccentric father and my soft-spoken, invalid mother, who seemed to be barely alive after all her protracted illnesses. There had been the family's good name and its struggle to survive. And suddenly all of that was gone, all the colour and light. After the second operation there was a quiet funeral. Ariadna knotted her hair at her nape and pinned a piece of crepe to her hat. Papa turned grey, skinny, and became utterly mad, but he was a happy madman whose laughter often turned to tears. The servant was let go, and strangers moved in with us. I started running out to the cooperative and to the bread distribution centre on the way to the Warsaw Railway Station, where sometimes you could get milk.

That long winter of 1920 brought the three of us together in one room, which had once been the dining room. In the middle of this room stood a cast-iron stove. Our life revolved around that stove, which gave out a slow heavy warmth in the evenings. Father groaned and chuckled and told jokes behind his screen. At that time they still made me laugh, but Ariadna didn't even smile with her eyes. He dressed and undressed behind that screen, read, slept and muttered to himself. Sometimes when we were in that room it seemed as if Ariadna and I were the only people in the entire world. Especially in the evenings, when she and I went to bed on the deep leather sofa that had been in Father's study. Various pieces of furniture had been brought in from each room. We lay with our heads at opposite ends, each covered up with her own blanket. And as everything died down and the last flame flickered behind the grate, chasing and shaking the shadows on the white wall, I fell asleep hugging her knees.

I warmed them. I held them close, close to

my strong childish chest. I had conversations with them, conversations I couldn't have with Ariadna herself. I told them stories, I whispered my dreams to them, I called them pet names. She would stir in her sleep, shift away from me and come back again. A white spot from some light—maybe the streetlamp, or the moon — flickered in the corner of the ceiling above Father's screen. I cried softly; I laughed from happiness. I feared life and believed in it. I wanted something grand and yet felt very small. I always came first, and no one needed me.

The long, almost seamless night merged into a long, almost seamless day. We went to bed when it was still light and awoke to bright May sunshine. Yes, she was grown up now. That year she grew up. Her arms were gently rounded, and her slender face was longer. She was so thin that when she undressed to bathe (and I stood on a stool and poured water over her) I could see all her bones move beneath her skin. Her pink-blue breasts moved too, either vanishing completely (when she raised her arm, for instance) or reappearing (when she leaned over).

On the evenings Father was not at home we were especially quiet and industrious. We took baths, washed out our shirts and slips, shampooed and trimmed each other's hair, made over old dresses, darned stockings. Sometimes we dug into a trunk and came up with an old jacket or a funny, old-fashioned cape, and Ariadna would try it on and walk around the room looking at herself in the mirrors. Then she would forget she was wearing it and without taking it off proceed to think up new hairdos for herself and for me, attach buckles to a worn-out pair of shoes or play with faded ribbons. She tried to picture the wondrous masked ball in her imminent future. Her life was about to start. Not this dull, miserable, half-starved life but another life, a life that had yet to begin. She would put her arm out to one side, throw her head back, and deliver a magnificent, non-sensical monologue that would make tears glisten in her eyes and roll down my cheeks. No matter what she did then – she was eighteen that summer – it meant just one thing: somewhere there was life. Somewhere there was the rapture of happiness and the tyranny of fate, and you had to be ready for anything when the doors to the light- and music-filled ballroom were flung open.

Usually Father came home from work late and ate a bowl of kasha, washing it down with black tea. No bread, no sugar. Sometimes we were both asleep by then and he woke us up with his heavy boots, the soles tied on with string, that were forever just about to come apart. Every so often he would walk over to our sofa and look at Ariadna, at me, and back at Ariadna. She would open her light blue eyes, slip her hand with its transparent little ring between her cheek and the pillow, and say, 'Oh, Papa!' in a kind of doleful reproach. But he was ready to settle into his easy chair and trundle out one of his strange stories, which more often than not began like this:

'Mark Twain once said to me, "Listen, mister, I forget your name and patronymic . . ."'

In September Ariadna got a job in a museum, and I was alone for entire days at a stretch. Indefatigable, I slaved away from the moment she walked out the door. I washed the floor, stood in lines, picked up our rations, cooked and did the laundry. Sometimes when I couldn't lift the big kettle of borscht or the cauldron of boiling linen I asked old Countess Rydnitskaya, whose hair was cut short like a man's and who always had a pipe clenched between her teeth, to come in from the next room and help me. In each room of our apartment – there were five altogether – a separate family lived with its own stove and laundry and children. Only the Countess lived by herself. She was waiting for permission to go back home, but her papers still had not come.

After breakfast Father went to work, and I went back to my scrubbing and mopping, holding my childish imagination in check between tough dried fish and mouldy millet. Then I went to see the Countess and listen to her stories of a gay, lavish, fairy-tale world of moustached men, lace stoles, fur muffs and the Virgin Mary.

At six Ariadna and I had our supper.

'If only you'd read some Pushkin,' she told me. 'It would be good to send you to school. We could pay the Countess to make dinner for us.'

Then I knew that this muddled life of mine was about to end, that I was going to start learning. At ten I was strong, my hands red, my voice rough. I wore a wool cap with ear flaps and felt boots, and the sole purpose of my childish existence was to lay my hands on something edible and bring it home.

When Ariadna came home from work she undressed, sat down at the table, and looking straight ahead, began telling me about her day. She worked in a back room of the museum where books were kept and there was always something being packed or unpacked, far from where the pictures were hanging and people walked about. Her rations were quite good: tobacco, herring, sometimes lard or groats. I had to take the sled when I went to pick them up. How eagerly I harnessed myself to it! How briskly I tramped over the icy pavement, across the steep bridge over the Ekaterinsky Canal, pulling at my nose and tossing my braid behind my ear!

I already knew Georgy Serafimovich, her boss, and Vera Sergeevna, her co-worker, and the other museum workers, as they were now called, who came to see Ariadna from time to time – Professor Maximov, the palaeontologist Grize, and the poet Andrei Zvonkov. I had a very precise picture in my mind of the big room where Ariadna sat next to a tall window and made entries in an oversized ledger in her round, back-slanting script. Vera Sergeevna sat opposite and wore a silk top. Everyone was in love with her. She knew every writer in Petersburg and went to the theatre every night. And Georgy Serafimovich in his cap and galoshes – he was well educated and never satisfied with anything – crawled among the boxes of antiquities, forever cursing and threatening to go to Moscow and lodge a complaint.

At the time it seemed to me that the life we were leading, that everyone around us was leading, in this, the only city in the world (because I had no conception of other cities), that this life of ours with its constant, gnawing hunger, its cold, its torn sheets and its hole-filled shoes, the black soot of the stoves and the gloom in the streets, the ice, the dread of winding up an orphan, of prison, of beggary, the separations and the hospitals, was the only life there was. Just as I couldn't imagine an orange or a seashore I'd never seen, so I couldn't believe then that there were such things as frivolous presents, aimless walks, spending money, or peace and quiet.

Meanwhile, Countess Rydnitskaya visited us from time to time and told Ariadna and me stories about fur muffs and lace stoles. She grieved over us – over me because I'd never know 'life's golden dawning', as she put it, and over Ariadna because her life was slipping by without that vague poetry which the Countess held so dear.

'My poor little girls,' she would say, puffing away at her pipe. 'My poor spring flowers.'

Ariadna, saddened by this, chewed on her sparkling ring. But I guffawed just as crudely and loudly as I did at my father's jokes, though I did have a feeling (which I never admitted to anyone) that in part she was right, not entirely, but a little. That feeling made me afraid that my laughter would turn into tears.

Two young girls visited us as well, the Dyukova sisters, Lyuda and Tata. They were big, buxom, pretty girls, Ariadna's friends from school. At first they didn't trust me and made me cover my ears at the most interesting parts of their conversation, but eventually they got used to me.

'That Sasha! Oh, that Sasha!' they chorused, and even Ariadna chimed in sometimes, 'Oh, that Sasha of mine!'

And that 'oh' referred to my fearlessness, to my smart rejoinders, to my acquisitive eyes and my strong hands, which latched on tight to anything and everything.

She was many times better than Lyuda or Tata, my Ariadna, with her big eyes, pale hair, fragile build, and her heart which was like nobody else's, or so it seemed to me at the time. Listening to their conversations, usually conducted in alternating whispers and laughter, it dawned on me that one of the

Dyukovas was planning to get married, that is, planning to move out of her parents' house, away from her sister, and live with some stranger, having registered with him first, of course, at the commissariat. And what was the reason behind this whole calamity? Her love for that stranger, who apparently was not so young, and his love for her, which they spoke of chiefly in whispers on our couch. It also dawned on me that the other Dyukova was in love with someone too, and was meeting extraordinary obstacles in her attempts to be united with him. The thought that Ariadna might marry some day and leave us, leave me alone with my father, alone to the cheerless gloom of my life, horrified me. I started to keep special watch over her, and what I saw frightened me.

What I saw was creeping indifference towards us, as if her thoughts were otherwise occupied. She came home later and left earlier. She started going out in the evening, and she never told me what she did. She started sleeping differently — her breathing couldn't fool me. Even her face looked different.

I remember one of the first Sundays of the new year of 1922. We were all still together. Father was writing something at his desk, and from time to time he would look calmly in our direction and say something mad, and we would exchange bewildered looks. We were sitting on the couch – Ariadna in the middle, Lyuda and Tata to either side of her, and I on one side or the other trying to perch on an arm, though they kept pushing me off and once even set me down on the floor.

'There are animals, girls,' said Papa, 'who can pull their intestines out through their own navels and play beautiful melodies on them.'

I looked at Ariadna.

'Why do you keep looking at me?' she demanded. 'Lyuda, give her a push. Why does she keep looking at me that way? If only you'd read some Pushkin! When you screw your eyes up your face looks so plain. You're going to be so ugly when you grow up!'

Tata laughed, wound my braid around her hand and said, 'Ugly but practical – and very mad.'

'Practical and mad, like her late lamented father,' Papa raised a cold-blooded voice from behind his paper.

But I kept watching her, and fear of the future – hers and mine – gripped me, a fear which I could share with no one. I tried to squeeze in between them again, and finally they let me, tickled me, covered my face with a cushion. And I kept trying to understand why I loved her so much. Why was I so afraid of losing her? Why did I want to be near her always?

I remember that evening. It was the evening before that amazing night when we were finally alone. Father snored behind his screen, the stove had gone out long before and the room was cold. The upright piano on which Lyuda had banged out a Chopin waltz had been left open and showed its white keys, and every so often something would shift in the stack of dirty dishes. (I didn't have the energy to wash all those cups and saucers so late.)

I hugged her cold skinny legs and asked softly, 'Do you like them? Do you like them a lot?'

'Who? The Dyukovas?'

'Do you tell them *everything*?'

She stirred. 'I don't tell anyone everything.'

'I'd like someone to tell everything to. Wouldn't you?' I could tell she was tempted to brush me off with a joke, a tease, but she refrained.

'Tell me everything,' she said.

'I can't. I will if you will too.'

Suddenly she reached under the blanket and gave my fingers a gentle squeeze. 'Why aren't you older, Sasha?' she said, almost out loud. 'You'd be my best, my closest friend.'

I gasped and froze.

'What about now?'

'Now all I've got is Tata and Lyuda. Later, only much later, I'll have you. Oh, I don't know. Maybe it's better like this. You know, there are times in your life when you don't need girl friends.'

'Don't you need me?'

'You're my sister. All of a sudden you start needing something completely different, something special and serious. Everything else seems so childish.'

I sat up in bed. 'Are you in love?' I cried out in horror. Tears gushed down my face and hands.

'Calm down! What's come over you! You'll wake Papa. Come here. Lie down next to me.'

I crawled over to her, and we were still for a while. She'd never asked me to lie next to her before. I was so happy that way, so untroubled – even in the darkest corners deep down inside. Right then I wanted only one thing: for that night to go on forever. A warmth came from Ariadna, a dear soapy fragrance from her neck, and something sweet-smelling from her hair. She lay stretched out next to me in her long, high-collared, long-sleeved nightgown, and I could feel her shoulder, her knee.

'Tell me who he is,' I said, light-headed from bliss and terror.

'Who is he? Oh, that's not so easy to say,' she replied as if to herself, for herself. 'He works in the theatre. He wants to write for the theatre. He wants to be a director. But he's married, so we're just going to live together.'

I didn't really understand what she was saying, but I didn't want to interrupt to ask.

'Papa will never allow it, naturally. He doesn't have a real job or a ration card. Anyway, he's kind of odd, very special, and terribly ugly. You'll see.'

'Does he love you?'

She sighed a broken sigh.

'Yes, Sasha,' and suddenly she pulled away from me. 'He loves me and I love him. And we've decided to be together.'

When we were both quiet you could hear her heart and mine pounding in counterpoint under the blanket.

We fell asleep together, and that night I had a dream.

I forget what the dream was about, but it left a mood, a sense of anxiety, a melancholy that ran through it, from the first time the stranger appeared in our room, between the stove and screen, to when he vanished in the unfamiliar back streets of a city that looked like Petersburg. I lost the point of the dream, although probably there wasn't one, as in most dreams. All that remained of it was a strange aftertaste, a mysterious knot that weighs on me to this very day. That man, who in my dreams was called Ariadna's husband and around whom the whole complicated mechanism of my childish dreaming revolved, was bound up in some incomprehensible way with our entire existence, with the collapse of Russia, with the hard, brutal, grievous things that happened in our waking hours. It was as if he bore some inexplicable and horrible relation to Mama's death, and the cold, and the hunger, and my older brother's recent execution, and Countess Rydnitskaya's troubles.

His name was Sergei Sergeevich Samoilov, and when I saw him for the first time it was dark – the dark of winter that had begun long before and would end much later – and Ariadna was getting ready to go to a concert, tying the strings of her hood in front of the mirror. Papa watched her silently and morosely, but she was all rosy, in full bloom, telling first him and then me one silly thing after another and pacing about in her felt boots. When the bell finally rang in the hall she told us in a low voice that her friend, Sergei Samoilov, had come for her. He was Andrei Zvonkov's friend, a poet, and a good friend of Vera Sergeevna.

'A beau?' asked Papa, and there was something nasty in his face.

At this first meeting it suddenly became clear to me how much Ariadna had broken away, from our father's and mother's military background into that rootless avant-garde associated with the university, museums, literary gatherings and experimental theatres. The conjunction of all our misfortunes, great and small, had led her to the expanses of a different life, had led her to Samoilov, and Papa seemed to understand that then, too. Smiling, she greeted Samoilov and introduced him to Father. I stood motionless behind the stove, in the corner near the cupboard, and watched them, completely absorbed.

Samoilov was nearly thirty then. He was blond, round-shouldered and red-nosed. His teeth were bad, and there was an intelligent look in his bright eyes. He was a young man with no sign of breeding or of any awareness of other people. He had a way of speaking without listening to anyone else and of coming and going when he pleased. He didn't maintain the proper physical distance between himself and other people, and there was something obstinate in his hunched-up shoulders and sloping forehead. He wore a thick grey quilted vest and quilted coat and did not remove his peaked cap right away. He stood there and waited for Ariadna to pull on her mittens.

'I must warn you quite frankly,' my father told him after a minute had passed, 'so that you are under no false impression: one of her eyes is glass. My poor Ariadna, what a nasty thing happened to her in her childhood! But it's so well done that you can't tell which one isn't real.'

Samoilov looked at him with curiosity.

'So, then, and what do you do, Comrade Samsonov?' Papa asked, smiling sweetly all of a sudden, all ready to sit in his chair and have a cosy chat.

But Samoilov and Ariadna were set to go out. Her face was unrecognisable. It shone.

'I'm thinking about putting on some little plays, various kinds of plays, in a theatre I know, and take it to the people,' Samoilov replied in all seriousness. 'I'm trying my hand at different kinds of comic skits. I'm giving my all – and I've not done too badly, even if I do say so myself. I adore any kind of poetic presentation.'

I was standing in my corner, behind the cupboard, and looked at him, wide-eyed.

'But who is this? A little girl or a little boy?' he asked suddenly when he saw me, and pointed a finger in my direction.

'A girl,' I answered loudly.

'So, you must be Irochka or Kirochka, right?' he continued, without the slightest softening in his voice.

'No, I'm Sasha,' I said firmly.

'How do you do, Sasha,' he replied with a sudden curtness. He walked over to me very quickly and shook my hand. A minute later they were both gone.

'How do you do, Samoilov,' I said proudly, but I don't know whether he heard me. Father didn't look in my direction. He picked up a fragile blue glass that we kept by the wash basin where we brushed our teeth and threw it at the mirror over the mantel. There was a terrible crash. The glass broke into tiny pieces, showering the entire room, but somehow the mirror was left intact and everything looked the same in it: the murk, the lamp clouded in smokiness, our silvery wallpaper, the slanted, closed door. Then Father went

behind his screen, lay down on his bed and
started laughing very loudly – or crying. I
could never tell his laughing from his crying.
Later that night the mirror shattered.

For a long time I couldn't sleep. Countess
Rydnitskaya sat by my feet and knitted a
scarf, a lilac scarf with tassels. I watched her
and felt like crying and telling her all about it,
but I was brave and said nothing.

'So, my wonderful little girl,' said the
Countess, 'that evening, for the first time,
he and I went to the islands. The driver
waited downstairs. I was wearing a gauze
dress the colour of champagne, with an
open neck and a diamond and amethyst
pendant. At that time women wore curls on
top of a chignon. Each curl was perfumed,
and a comb was stuck in on top, a very,
very fancy carved comb, and with paste
jewels as well.'

She left, and for a long time I stared at the
place where she had sat and I waited for
Ariadna. But I fell asleep before she came in. I
woke up when I felt someone getting in with
me under the blanket. Her hands were shaking, and so was her whisper.

'Sasha, Sasha,' she whispered. 'Time to
sleep, Sasha. Are you asleep? Why not? You
have to sleep. Give me a hug, Sasha. What's

wrong? Don't mind me. I don't know what's happening to me either.'

But I wasn't going to hug her any more, and I wasn't going to cry with her. That night I had hardened, and I even experienced a certain satisfaction from feeling harder. I curled up and moved closer to the wall, feigning sleep.

In the daytime everything was the same as ever: laundry, cleaning, standing in lines, going out to buy sugar from the dealers in the third courtyard of a building on Marat Street, carrying firewood up from the cellar where someone was pilfering it, and my tears over the missing logs, the harsh, cold, unbearably rough, dark life, the third winter – the longest, the saddest. In the daytime everything was just the same: 'If only you'd read some Pushkin,' and Father's soft hand resting on the table as he wrote or ate or just sat and stared into space. But at night everything was different. Ariadna went out almost every day, or rather, she no longer came home after work. Instead she came in late, when we were both already asleep, and sometimes I didn't even wake up when she came in.

But once, in early March (I remember, it was the first thaw; I'd caught a cold and was staying at home with a muffler wound around my neck), on one of those evenings when Father wasn't home, Samoilov came to see Ariadna again, for the second and last time. He wasn't alone. With him were Zvon- kov and Vera Sergeevna, and the four of them drank tea which I heated on the stove, ate black bread, smoked and talked.

There was a semblance of cosiness in our room that evening. The shattered mirror had been replaced by a bright, cheerful picture which Ariadna had been given by an artist friend. There was a new home-made shade on the lamp. A clean tablecloth was spread on the table, and there was a big dried pink flower in the vase – you couldn't tell whether it was real or imitation.

'This is Sasha,' Ariadna told each of them in turn, pointing to me, and I clumsily stuck out my red hand.

Later I quietly undressed and lay down, and the guests paid no attention to me, shouted, nibbled on crusts of bread with their tea, recited poems, argued. It was as if Ariadna were her old self again, though the cigarette in her slender hand and a peculiar curl over one ear were a surprise that made my heart contract. Tall, flat-chested, slant- eyed, but nonetheless in her own way beauti- ful, Vera Sergeevna spoke least of all, but it was clear to me that she was in charge of the conversation. Zvonkov and Samoilov used the familiar 'you' with each other. Zvonkov recited several poems, and I guessed that they were all his own. He read them in a sing-song voice, which made the poems sound wonderful to me, and when he stopped, Samoilov started to talk about something, also in a slight sing-song tone – and then it got quiet and they listened to him, but he broke off without finishing, saying that God hadn't given him an ear, hadn't given him the gift. He could invent anything at all, but he couldn't rhyme two lines. At the same time, he clearly had something on his mind that he wanted to bring to life, that tormented him, that had been maturing, perhaps for a long time, an image for which he had already found a name: the tattered cloak.

'It was dug out of an old trunk that had taken root in the floor of Grandfather's house. It smelled of camphor and looked terribly big to us, but in the old days men must have been more substantial than we are. See, it's full of holes! It's completely out of fashion. But although it's badly motheaten, it's still splendid. You could wrap yourself up in it from head to toe and keep out the cold. It needs an airing. It's been lying too long at the bottom of the trunk.

'Many years ago our fathers, in the forests of Manchuria at the approaches to Port Arthur, wrapped you and me up in this cloak. We were children, and we were cold out on the Korean steppes. Our fathers never came back. Our mothers came back with us alone. Our grey-eyed, fair-haired mothers raised us, and when Russia's troubles came they couldn't bear the summers or the winters. We buried them and set plain wooden crosses over them.

'We've seen a lot. We've never been afraid. But a lot more lies ahead of us. We've forgotten our prayers and life has stolen away our hopes. Nothing will ever bring them back. You've wrapped your dainty feet up in this old cloak so many times, and I've draped it over myself more than once, trying to cheer you up by pretending I was Childe Harold of old. Tell me, wasn't this the cloak Joseph wrapped round Mary and the infant on their journey into Egypt? Or maybe it's Don Quixote's cloak? Or perhaps it belongs to the god himself, Cervantes? Remember how we wrapped his wounded arm in it and covered his blinded eyes with it, and how we ran after him, weeping, but by then he couldn't see us? Or is this the cloak of Lear struggling through the storm we've known so well for so long?

'Now times are different. I must go one way and you another. We'll rip this old cloak in two. It's gone out of style anyway. It reminds me of an old-fashioned pelerine, but that's all right. I'm leaving for good, for the open spaces of my gloomy and cruel land, not because I love it but because for me there is no other road. Farewell!

'You take the other half of this two thousand-year-old garment of ours. You run away from here, from me, from us. Run and don't look back, my sweet one, my love. Run over the seas and the mountains, run to other lands. Do not fear loneliness, do not fear your orphanhood. Live like a bird, perhaps the wind. Safeguard your young and tender life. Run away — to Africa, Australia, Asia. Pick one of the two Americas. Run away from these sad and awful places —

'The tattered cloak to shield
Your young and lovely face.'

I'd probably started a fever. I listened to Samoilov's high-pitched voice. He rocked ever so slightly as he spoke, sometimes trying to couch a line in iambic trimeter. I remember him saying, 'There is no other road,' and then, at the end, 'one of the two Americas.' But he couldn't write verse, and naturally his poem would never be written. None the less, in the semidark of that room so full of smoke and heat it somehow did take on a precise form for a few moments, because after Samoilov fell silent his three listeners and the fourth (which was myself) could still hear the flow and rhythm of his unrealised poem inside us.

'That's good,' said Zvonkov, 'very good. Why don't you give it to me?'

'It's yours. Do what you like with it,' Samoilov responded.

Then there was a silence that seemed endless to me, when I could hear a pounding and ringing in my ears.

It was the stinging wind cutting me in the face. I see Petersburg of those years like a sketch traced in the snow. By a steep stone footbridge at the juncture of two frozen canals I see a big poster tacked up: in this theatre, Samoilov's play is being performed for the two thousandth time. The wind whips the poster and it tears, like the old cloak. Through the holes in the cloak you can see the red sunset. A poem about a red sunset is being recited in a smoke-filled room. Some-

one is garbling it – deliberately, insisting on
his mistakes, and pale, slant-eyed Vera Sergeevna is correcting Zvonkov, but he is insis-
tent:

> But we the heirs of Blok
> Are helpless to forget.

What are we helpless to forget? The cold
clinic where Mama died? Or the dense, grey,
clay-like hunk of our daily bread? Or that
green and lonely star over Senate Square last
May? I take that star to sleep with me as if I'd
stolen it.

Later that night I opened my eyes. The light
was on in the room. Father was standing in
his shirt and underclothes, hanging on to the
screen and saying something in a very loud
voice. Ariadna was sitting at the table, tous-
led and pink, her arms stretched across the
table. There was indescribable disarray in the
room. I stirred and closed my eyes again.

'If his intentions are honourable, he
shouldn't be furtive. Let him come. Let him
marry you,' said Father, evidently repeating
the same words for the tenth time. 'Where did
you get involved with him? Where are you
running off to? What kind of man is he,
anyway? No, answer me, what kind of man is
he? An actor? A stagehand? An acrobat,

maybe? Does he work on a trapeze? Has anyone bothered to explain to me who it is I'm dealing with?'

She snatched a breath, as if for him.

'I'm going to go and live with him soon,' she said calmly. 'We're going to live together, as he's married.'

Father let out an 'Ah!' and it became very quiet in the room. That frightened me. I opened my eyes and sat up on the bed. At that moment I felt no more love for anyone in the world, and Ariadna seemed like a total stranger to me. Stunned by that revelation, I looked around me and burst into noisy tears.

She had noticed the change in me. The next evening – the last evening of her life with us – she and I found ourselves alone together, like old times, and she gathered her things into a canvas duffel bag and barely spoke to me. She avoided me, not explaining her departure, as if it should all have been clear to me without that. I was standing by the window.

'How can you go out in that snow?' I asked.

Fat, wet flakes were falling on the street.

'It's all right, it's not far,' she replied. 'What time is it?'

It was ten minutes to ten.

'Give this letter to Papa.'

I felt something powerful stir inside me. 'Aren't you ever going to come here again?' I asked. 'What about me?'

'Enough, enough. Don't be such an idiot. You're going to come and visit me.'

'That's not true. That's never going to happen.'

Suddenly she sat down and hid her face in her hands.

'I realised,' she said, as if she were trying to justify something to herself, at the same time aware that I was the wrong person to listen to words like that, 'I realised that this isn't life.' She indicated our room. 'Not you, not him.' She pointed to the screen. 'Life is something absolutely, totally different. It's nothing like this.'

'It's Samoilov and his tattered cloak,' I said rudely.

She smiled. 'Yes, it's the tattered cloak. Some day you'll remember me, and those words, and that whole evening, won't you, Sasha?'

'Don't go,' I said, barely audibly. 'Don't go, Ariadna. Make it be different.'

'I can't.'

I couldn't understand her. I sobbed at the cold window-sill, and she kissed my hair and held me close. I don't remember what happened after that: saying goodbye, her leaving me alone to the light of the lamp burning in the ceiling, the heart-breaking silence. Father came home later than usual. I jumped up to meet him. He stopped short two steps away from me.

'A letter,' I said. 'You have a letter from her, Papa.'

'Ah!' he said abruptly. 'And what might this letter be about?'

I felt my whole face tremble under his gaze.

'She's gone, Papa,' I stated finally.

'Ah! So why read a letter? If that's all, then there's nothing to read. It's the fact itself that's important. The fact is known. To hell with the letter.'

He kicked open the grating and thrust the letter into the burning stove. Without removing his cap, galoshes or snowy overcoat he went behind the screen, sprawled on his bed and was silent.

For a few days we hid our misfortune from everyone, but Countess Rydnitskaya finally came to see us.

'One must never do things like that,' she said, puffing on her pipe. 'Youth is flowers and love. Youth is beauty. This vulgar, crude life we lead is tearing off all the petals, killing off the tender shoots. Your father's tragedy simply defies description.'

I didn't understand a word she said, and that bothered me.

Ariadna lived nearby, on Razyezhaya, and I ran into her once or twice that year. She wore a velvet ribbon around her neck and a home-made leather hat. Each time she kissed me happily and excitedly and questioned me about our lives, and whether I was going to school, and did I remember her (as if I could forget her, as if I were five instead of eleven). She had lost a certain sensitivity to me and talked to me in the way that adults who aren't used to children talk to them. I began to hold back with her as well. I wanted to let her know that I wasn't the same little girl I'd been when I'd slept with her on our only sofa, that I was going to school, that I read books, that I had tasted life and understood quite a lot already. So we stood on the corner by the stationery shop and were deeply insincere with one another.

Later I did in fact start school. Ariadna moved across the river. And a year after that Papa's sister sent for us from France. Dressed in government-issue shoes, coats sewn from soldiers' greatcoats and shirts cut out of old sheets, we went to Paris, carrying a basket of tinware and a bundle of strapped-together pillows.

II

Paris. Paris. There is something silken and elegant about that word, something carefree, something made for a dance, something brilliant and festive like champagne. Everything there is beautiful, gay and a little drunk, and festooned with lace. A petticoat rustles at every step; there's a ringing in your ears and a flashing in your eyes at the mention of that name. I'm going to Paris. We've come to Paris. We're going to live in Paris. But what I saw my first day resembled neither silk nor lace nor champagne.

Imagine that a man has landed on the moon. He's expecting to see a majestic and menacing wasteland, dead mountains, stone chasms, a special sky. Suddenly he notices that he's looking at the stucco wall of his neighbour's house, it's raining and the courtyard stinks. When I looked out the window of our Paris apartment it seemed to me that everything was exactly as it had been at our old place: that feeling of being on the edge of a big city along with a multitude of poverty-stricken people, chiefly women, and chiefly old women at that; a quiet, murky street with the smoking chimney of a commercial laundry and a blue locksmith's sign; over the sign an open window with a torn tulle curtain and behind that an old man inserting a set of false teeth into his wide, wet mouth. Above it all there is a narrow stripe: a swatch of the local sky, grey and low. There, around the corner, and further – the same street again, desolate and impoverished, where an ugly little girl who looks a little like me is walking (or is that me walking with my butcher bag?). A joint of beef juts out of the bag, red and solid. A worker passes with a bottle of wine in the bulging pocket of his patched jacket. And then nothing, no one. All you hear is the pounding from the artificial sausage-casing factory. From time to time the din increases, which means they've opened the door to the street, and then the whole block, including our house, starts to smell of something rotten and astringent.

I lived on that street not one year, not three, not five, not even ten. I lived there for sixteen years of my life, looking out of those windows, breathing in the black fumes from the factory chimney. Those years were utterly indistinguishable: the swing of a pendulum forming a constant rectangle of time, from spring to summer and from autumn to winter, in the cell of which I listened with equal docility to the noise of the factory and the hush of Sunday. During those years things withered, rusted and faded around me; the locksmith's azure sign turned a duller blue. On the other hand, some things were renewed, scrubbed clean, freshly painted. But in our apartment – inside our house, where a Strauss waltz played on the radio day after day, where the ubiquitous cat played with her shadow day after day, where my father and I slept in our cramped room and put out folding cots end to end, like corpses in Russia, night after night – nothing ever changed. Everything held fast somehow, intending, surely, to disintegrate some day, perhaps after we were gone. Only we ourselves changed. Father's sister Varvara, who had sent for us and who seemed at first a fresh, forty-year-old woman who never lacked either work or a lover, in those years became an old woman, still doing daywork, going to other people's kitchens to wash dishes or mop floors. Her friends still came by in the evenings as they always had, but her lieutenants and captains were not as bold or assiduously groomed and pomaded as they had once been. No, they were old and meek, like Varvara herself, and they had the same big, rough worker's hands.

During the first seven years Father worked as a guard in a garage, and after that as a delivery boy in a pastry shop. Now he was out of work. In fact, he wasn't fit to work any more, and he had stopped trying to find a job. His stories were as mad as ever, without beginning or end, his laugh was more like a sob than ever, and he still liked to tease. Only now at the end of each story there came a tearful address to me, 'My child Cordelia! Daughter of mine!' And when I wasn't there, he said it into space, to where I ought to have been.

I, of course, changed more than anyone. I had been thirteen and I became twenty-nine. My whole youth was behind me, and I had nothing to show for it. Having been a plain little girl, angular and muscular, I became a plain young woman, stocky and pale. It didn't take long for me to lose what youthfulness I'd had, my freshness and high-cheekboned purity. Although quite healthy, I suddenly started to resemble my sickly mother, and my hands, once so deft, became large and white, like the hands of a peasant woman who has just given birth.

I had been thirteen and now I was almost thirty. But sometimes it seemed to me that I was just the same as before, that I had never learned anything, never mastered anything, never discovered anything here, that everything I had inside me I'd already had in me there: my knowledge of the world, the despair of loneliness, my secret lofty sentiments, my tears, my thoughts and the fortitude I hid from everyone. All those things I had brought with me, all those things had been given to me back in Russia, and I remained what I had always been.

Meanwhile, my life had worked out no worse or better than other lives. That voracious scramble for a bite to eat and a warm corner had ended. In this new city you could live like a human being: work, earn your keep, make ends meet. At first I went to school, but after a few years I had to give it up for lack of time. I had to help out at home. Varvara was sewing then, and for quite a while I worked for her. It was from her that I learned to iron, sew and work buttonholes, and in return she made me a dress once a year, a new dress out of some thick wool which I lovingly and secretly admired for months before getting to put it on.

When I turned twenty I started working as a presser in the commercial laundry on the corner. By that time Varvara's life had taken a turn for the worse. One sad winter Sunday just before Christmas she went out to wait at tables in a neighbourhood Russian restaurant and shortly afterwards took a regular job there. But a few months later she slipped and broke her leg while carrying a plate of oysters, and she was crippled for the rest of her life. That was when she started doing daywork in private homes.

I became a presser. In the course of nine years I ironed other people's sheets every day from morning to night, learning to stand on my feet for ten hours at a stretch. I earned a regular wage, and since by then I already knew that all pressers and laundresses put money aside – and not just them, but shop-girls and clerks and actors and even ministers – I too started saving. I liked this idea, of which I had had no conception before: save part of the money you earn by the sweat of your brow and then use that money to . . . but what exactly I would do with it I did not yet know.

At first I liked the wartime air of my aunt's apartment, so unlike that of our Petersburg caves. In the evenings, when guests sat at the tea table and all talked about how the next day they would sally forth and do battle, it seemed to me that the dispositions had already been made, that we were all bivouacked. 'The general has ordered the troops to assemble.' 'The gentlemen of the staff have decided.' 'The hussars are now on regimental leave.' That was all I heard. And I was surprised that these people with grey faces and rough hands didn't wear plumes and blue and lavender greatcoats, didn't click their spurs or rattle their sabres. They had their own closely knit, uniquely agreeable life: the Maria Ivanovnas, Evgenia Lvovnas and Irina Alexandrovnas didn't consort with other men. They had their dances and parties, their raffles, their traditional dinners, prayers and masses for the dead at which they prayed piously, vigorously thrusting out their bemedalled chests and joining in with the church choir. But more important were those intoxicatingly pointless conversations – which mattered only to them – about the retreat from Ekaterinoslav, the surrender of Perekop, and the evacuation of Sevastopol; Varvara, whose husband had been a bugler in the hussars and had died from wounds on the way to Constantinople in 1919, was one of the few living links in that rusty, odd-sounding chain.

Nine years. No, I can't believe it. Do things really happen like that? Why? Why, though I committed no crime, did I end up standing at an ironing board for nine years lifting a heavy iron? The first few days I came home and cried all night at the impossibility of fulfilling my own destiny. Then I stopped crying and came to the conclusion that the people around me were right: my work was clean and my job steady; my documents were in order; and my wage was sufficient for me to live in the way I was expected to. After all, I had no education, no looks and no talent, so what else could I possibly be good for?

And I saved. Never in all those years did I buy myself a single extra or unnecessary item. All the stockings, shoes, dresses and underwear I wore were the plainest possible, and I went for years without buying gloves or a hat. I brought enough into the house for myself and Father, and the little left over I kept in a thick book on the shelf above my bed, a cookbook that no one had used in a long time. I heard about people putting money away for an operation, for their teeth, for a trip to the seashore, for a new sideboard or simply for their old age. From the very outset I had the idea of going to Italy one day. I didn't know quite what I was going to see in Italy – paintings, or cities, or just its dark nights and orange groves, the cypresses in its cemeteries. But I had a feeling that one day my dream would come true. All by myself I would go to Italy, Genoa, Rome. Why? To see what I had never ever seen.

In all those years only one single time was I able to get away from that life. That was five years ago, when Cavalry Captain Golubenko proposed to me. Captain Golubenko, one of the most valorous of Varvara's visitors, was over forty and owned an electrical supply store. He was a dark, hirsute, lively man, at one time quite the daredevil and dragon-slayer, but now his passion was balalaika orchestras, Russian cooking and singing at the table.

'You can sit at the cash register,' he said. 'My partner Vasily Karlovich Perlovsky and I will carry you on our arms.'

I was supposed to pay for the privilege of sitting rather than standing for the rest of my life, and pay with my freedom.

'Thank you for the honour,' I said as gently as possible, but it still came out rudely, 'but I must decline.' Where did I ever come up with that horrible word?

The next day Varvara asked me, 'Answer three questions for me, please. One, why did you refuse Golubenko? Two, what bastard are you sleeping with? And three, do you have any intention of ever settling down with a husband and, if so, what kind?'

'My child Cordelia! Daughter of mine!'

I thought conscientiously for a minute or two.

'One,' I said, 'because Golubenko is poor. Two, I'm not sleeping with any bastard. And three, I won't marry anyone who's not rich.' That said, I went to the corner and turned my back on both of them, took the cookbook off the shelf and counted my money. I had three thousand, three hundred and seventy francs.

Varvara went into the next room and there made that characteristic sound I knew so well: not exactly laughing, but not exactly crying either. It was something she and Father had in common. They looked alike, too. She called to me from the next room. Had I ever experienced any sort of love?

'What's love?' I asked. And suddenly I remembered Ariadna, and instead of going to Italy I felt like sending her all my savings.

All the time I'd lived in Paris one memory had lived on inside me; it breathed, changed shape, grew, intensified, subsided, melted and burst into life again. It gave me no rest. Often it made me happy; it let me know that there can be genuine and kind relations between people. It showed me the joy of intimacy with someone who until then had been a stranger but who touched your heart for eternity and was reflected in that heart, where he remained. This memory was very brief. It was a voice that once said to me gravely: 'How do you do, Sasha.' It was a look that once fell on me and had adhered. There were nights in my miserable existence when I lived for this memory, lighting upon and dwelling on it, sometimes gaily, sometimes tearfully.

It seemed to me that ever since my childhood I'd been a little in love with Ariadna, and now I could be in love with her lover. It seemed to me that I unconsciously wanted to compete with her and imitate her, or else that all this was just my curiosity about her life, about their fate, curiosity about his unrealised poetry, which certainly ought to have had a continuation. Gradually and imperceptibly the image of Samoilov became linked inside me with everything unattainable and wonderful in life, things I could only guess at, the world as it might have been but wasn't for me, people as they might have been but as I would never know them, my secret conjectures that apart from everyday reality there was something else – an image, a melody. As if in the darkest, most brutish years of my existence the beauty and poetry of the world winked at me as they raced past and instantly vanished. No matter that Samoilov himself was ugly and not very kind, and had no talent for composing poems. (We hadn't heard anything here of his having made a name for himself, had we?) Through him I had caught a glimpse of something, the enchantment of another world flashed before me at a time when there seemed no possibility of any kind of enchantment in the world. There was also the warmth of the man who had leaned towards me for a moment when all around me was cold and miserable and people were frightened and mistrustful. His 'How do you do, Sasha,' and his advice to live like 'a bird, perhaps the wind', not to be afraid of anything, to wrap ourselves up in the two thousand-year-old cloak, our cloak, albeit ripped in two, remained with me throughout my Paris life. I won't hide the fact that the actual memory of his face and voice faded over the years and lost its childish power, but everything that that face, that voice, had once awakened was alive. It lived on and sometimes blossomed within me.

This memory possessed no solidity or continuity. In my small, awkward soul it was sometimes absent for weeks and then suddenly stung me for no apparent reason, or began weakly, looming dreamily in my thoughts, and then it was gone. On especially lonely nights – when my father slept soundly next to me with his eyes wide open, talking to himself (that was the only way he slept those days) and on the other side of the wall Varvara's guests – they were all grey now, bald, toothless and wheezy – drank and sang (vodka, a guitar) with the same women friends (some long since grandmothers) at a Christmas party – or later, in the spring, it would descend upon me, uncoil, cast a spell over me and leave me in blissful thrall, on the verge of tears.

It was late August 1939, and of the three of us I was the only one who had a job. Father sat for days on end at the table and laid out hands of solitaire, paced from room to room hugging the walls, looked with fixed eyes but didn't see, listened but didn't hear. Coming upon the evening paper in a corner, he would read it for a long time and then say, barely mustering up the words, 'We can't give in. We'll simply have to fight. We'll all go. The main thing is showing some muscle.'

Varvara, mumbling away, mended and darned, washed and cooked; she was always out of work in August but could never reconcile herself to the fact. She was always grumbling, always cursing the summer and her own uselessness. A Strauss waltz boomed over the radio. It was hot, dull and dusty in the deserted city, and there I was standing and ironing, standing and ironing by a white wall, by a white table, wearing a white apron, alongside others exactly like me, old and young, puffed up and dried out, taciturn and talkative pressers who, like me, earned four francs an hour.

Time stood still. The warm smell of starched linen lingered static among us. The heat of the stove where the irons were heated, the red flush of our faces, the hissing of the irons, their quick tap on the edge of the board and, at quiet moments, the ticking of the clock over the boss's desk: all this was static. Certainly it had been like that for many years, and it was likely to remain so for ever. We cleaned up in the laundry at six-thirty, and at seven we went home. Staggering with weariness, dragging my swollen feet, I covered the few hundred paces that separated me from home. Women poured out of the sausage-casing factory towards me, and each of them was like me in some way, or so it seemed at the time.

They poured out towards me that day, their faces different, transformed by fear and worry. A radio snarled from a small café, but no one stopped to listen. Each already knew what she would hear.

'Here it comes again,' someone said, hanging out of a window, and the man standing on the street below replied, 'Here it comes again. It'll be the same thing all over again.'

The men's dismay and the women's terror made them all look alike. The old were tossed back into life, and the onrush of emotions made them young again; the young were transported by despair, which aged their pinched, darkened faces. The hot evening overhead came to a complete halt and stopped breathing, and on our street, in the twilight, someone wept loudly in the entry-way of a large grey apartment house.

In the evening after supper I went outside again, and for three evenings – through to Sunday – I went for a walk. At the corner of the rue Vaugirard, under a group of plane trees (there had been plans for a square, but they were dropped), a handful of Varvara's friends clustered and spoke quietly in Russian: Musya Meshcherskaya, Petrov, von Moor, Uncle Drozd in his navy overalls, Madame Churchurazova and her feebleminded daughter (both bareheaded and in slippers), Vasya Vostronosov, Petya Poleshatov and others, they too looking either a little older or a little younger. They called each other by their first names and called me Alexandra Evgenievna, as if I were from a different regiment. For three evenings we stood there, and on Sunday I circled through the sobbing, moaning, shouting streets and ended up at the train station, where no one paid anyone any attention, no one reacted to anyone else, and people, drunk with grief, crushed one another in the moving crowd and farewell embraces, stuffing themselves into the heavy, overloaded trains.

But the sky was still exactly the same. And I had the feeling then that a new page was not being turned that evening. No, it was as if someone had gone back through half the book, whipping back through more than twenty-five years with a swish and with a heavy hand dragging all of us back into dreadful, boring repetitions. We had fallen

into the same trap. The shutter had snapped
shut. Only a moment ago this or that had
both been possible, and now it was finished –
it had crushed us, knocked us down and
slammed shut.

Like everyone else that winter, I was stuck
in my lonely indifference. I had less and less
opportunity to save, being the sole breadwinner in the house now. Father was ill, Varvara
was getting old and almost never went out to
do daywork she was so busy with Father and
the house. Like the true breadwinner that I
was, I came home from work to find everything done for me. What kind of Italy could
there be now anyway? What kind of dreams
could anyone have? They withered in the
airless expanse of my continuous twilight.
For two decades, half-childish thoughts had
been enough for me. When Ariadna left us,
ever since the last time I saw Samoilov, it was
as if a star had gone out but its light had been
travelling towards me from an infinitely long
way away. Now I knew, according to the
precise law whereby all things come to an
end, that the light would go out.

It was during the June catastrophe that
Papa died, as if he couldn't bear what was
happening, although, what did it matter to
him, and vice versa? Then I took the money

out of the cookbook. About half of what was there went towards his funeral. Varvara, hot and puffy-faced, dishevelled, unwashed, stood there and took my notes in her outstretched hand, dumbstruck. Then she sat down on my bed and her tears gushed – not over Father but over me, as I understood her, through her sob-laced words.

'She saved! She saved! How did she find the will-power? She hasn't got a warm coat for the winter and never takes a holiday, but she saved! What are you, French or something? Where did you get that? There you have it, the younger generation. Machines, not people. No passion or abandon, all reason and calculation. But us, what about us? Yes, we certainly did know how to live! We never gave a thought to tomorrow. Never put anything in a bank. They're different now. They know about rainy days. When I was your age I ran fast and loose. Well, you won't have to bury your father in a common grave after all. She saved! Hear that, Evgeny, my friend? That Sasha of ours saved!'

He lay in a ray of sunshine, and there was something noble in his face now that had somehow been lacking before. A light edging ran between his eyelids and his tightly bound mouth. His legs were tied together, too, as were his hands. The effect was that of an ancient mummy. 'My child Cordelia! Daughter of mine!' he had whispered to me the evening before, and that memory made me cry, because every time he said that I knew he was remembering Ariadna. On his chest we found a baptismal cross and a worn locket that held two photographs – my mother and Ariadna – probably put there back in Russia. I put the locket on, along with the cross, and for a few days it annoyed, as it caught at my brassière.

His funeral was quite out of the ordinary. One bright sunny morning a hearse, a nag and two attendants from the bureau appeared. They loaded the coffin on to the hearse with the help of the concierge, and then both of them sat up front and suggested that Varvara and I sit on the sides, which we did. We rode at a jog trot, holding onto the coffin and tucking our feet underneath us and the whole time thanking God that everything had worked out as it had. There wasn't a soul on the streets of Paris, if you didn't count German guards. For some reason I remember especially well the square at the Church Montrouge, where there was no one to the right or the left, ahead or behind. The avenue du Maine was empty all the way to the

horizon, and the avenue d'Orléans was prist-
ine. All the doors and all the shops were
closed. It seemed to me that there were people
standing in windows pointing at us. At the
Port d'Orleans two German soldiers wearing
full battle dress and shifting from foot to foot
asked for our pass, after which we jog trotted
on. The boulevard Périphérique, absolutely
devoid of human life to the right and left,
reminded me of a movie I'd seen many years
before in which a scientist blanketed Paris in
instantaneous sleep, everything ground to a
halt and only the lovers on the uppermost
platform of the Eiffel Tower escaped.

The shutdown at the laundry lasted exactly
eleven days, after which everything started
up again – with the difference that now we
were doing laundry for German soldiers
rather than private clients. Soap and lye were
requisitioned, as was fuel, and the linen was
dropped off and taken away by truck.

We blundered into a winter without bread,
lard, wool or coal. Simple everyday house-
hold items around us gradually started to
wear out and break down, but there was
nothing to replace them with. The matches
wouldn't light any more – as in Russia once
upon a time – a sure sign of impending
disaster. Now it was just the two of us,

Varvara and I, and when I came home in the
evening there were two places set at our
three-legged kitchen table. We sat opposite
one another. She, nearly grey, heavy and
lame but still outlining her eyes in dark
pencil, was beginning to be ashamed of her
harmless little pleasures: drinking, smoking,
sitting for an evening by a darkened lamp-
shade with von Moor, who was himself now
quite bald and very ragged. Skinny but broad
in the bones, with hair of indeterminate
colour and a crudely asymmetrical face (the
left side was a little smaller than the right), I
always dressed in the same dark green skirt
and grey top, leafed through a library book
(Varvara's taste – a novel based on the lives
of counts and princes) or shuffled an old deck
of cards to lay out the only solitaire I knew
before Petrov and von Moor came and sat
down to a game of hearts.

Although her dark pudgy fingers were
swollen from the cold, Varvara still raised her
little finger high when she held her cup of
some suspicious concoction that smelled vaguely of camomile and pepper. The saccharine
in it fizzed because of the baking soda, and
ragged slices of stale bread spread with apple
butter completed the refreshments. Usually
everyone crowded into the tiny kitchen,

where it was warmer because there was gas. It was there, when the guests had gone, that we undressed, washed up as best we could over the grey basin, and ran, each to her own icy bed, where a hot water bottle rolled around under the covers. The guests emerged onto a dark staircase, struck matches and clapped their sides looking for a flashlight, only to find it and discover that the battery was dead – the property of all batteries, lamps and lighters in bad times. They emerged into the dark gloom of the street, where there wasn't a single light, into the urban gloom of the street, into the urban autumn night that was like a night in the forest or the fields – no fire, no voices, no shadows. When there was a moon, people were a little bolder. They took bigger steps and crossed the pavement with glad hearts. When it was raining you couldn't hear people coming, and sometimes two of you would collide head on – a stranger's repulsive warmth would touch your face, a stranger's weight would graze your body. When snow fell after the New Year it was brighter for a few nights from the white patches and the starry reflections. And you had to chide yourself, stepping around the drifts, groping around the corners of buildings, not to misjudge the intersection,

that this was Paris – silk, lace, champagne –
not Oboyan or Cheboksary torn between
Whites and Reds, not 1920 but 1940, 1941,
1942, and the earth was revolving around the
sun as before.

Even the conversation reminded me of my
Petersburg childhood. If on a lofty theme,
then it was inevitably about the fact that
nine-tenths of mankind were always half-
starved so we Parisians were only getting our
fair share. If not, then it was about where you
could get oil and when they would start
distributing potatoes. Hitherto indissoluble
knots unravelled with ease. The words
'arrest' and 'deportation' were bandied back
and forth like small change. And in that
shattered, hungry, cold life, any light of
memory, any ray of hope, died inside me.

That winter many people left, some to
work in Germany, others to fight in Russia,
others illegally to the South. Neither Musya
Meshcherskaya, the gypsy with the dangling
earrings, nor Petya Poleshatov, that bore, liar
and glutton, nor Uncle Drozd, the St Geor-
ge's Cross holder and cab driver, were among
our number any longer. Petrov and von
Moor kept coming, however. Both worked in
a repair shop attached to a garage the Germ-
ans had requisitioned, and they brought

either a head of cabbage or a kilo of sugar or simply a counterfeit bread ration card, all of which I paid for. If my wages didn't cover it, I took more money out of the cookbook.

Varvara limped from the kitchen to the bedrooms, sprinkling cigarette ash in the Lenten rutabaga pudding. The guitar Petrov loved to hold – he didn't play – hung in the kitchen. All three of them sat around the table on creaky chairs surrounded by brown walls and toasted each other with a little 'native brew', munched on pickles and drank eight cups of tea apiece. After she had had something to drink and smoke, Varvara laughed playfully, and they called her 'Barbishonchik', as they had forty years before. They even pretended to be jealous of one another. In any event, they took turns hugging her around the waist, squeezing her leg under the table and kissing her rough, pudgy fingers. Von Moor wielded notably greater rights over her than Petrov did. Meaningful, emotion-laden allusions sometimes popped up between her and von Moor, allusions that made Petrov sulk and strum the guitar strings.

'Come out here! We would be honoured by your presence!' they both exclaimed.

I had nowhere to hide in that chilly apartment, so I joined them in the kitchen because it was warm there.

'Alexandra Evgenievna, don't condemn us for behaving like children. As a certain Spaniard once said, "passion is life".'

I sat down between them. Scrawny little Petrov, with his awful, thick lips and sunflower-yellow eyes, kissed me on the shoulder, pretending to be drunk. Varvara, outraged, slapped him on the hand with her heavily perfumed and slightly grubby handkerchief.

There were two bottles on the table. Varvara liked to put old envelopes under them to protect the oilcloth. But this time, placed ingenuously underneath the bottle of red *ordinaire*, was an unopened letter addressed to me, and when I saw it it was already spotted with wine.

'Forgive me, Sasha. It's my fault, my fault!' cried Varvara. 'It's been there two days already, hidden under the bread. I kept forgetting to tell you.'

'The gas company?' Von Moor showed interest and gave a loud laugh.

'The tax collector,' Petrov replied and solicitously passed me a dirty fork to open the envelope.

The letter was very short. The longer you wait, the shorter the letter is. Actually, it ought to have consisted of one simple appeal: so many years . . .

'Dear Alexandra Evgenievna, I would like to see you. I've known for a long time that you are in Paris, too. Once I even caught a glimpse of you (two years ago). However, I don't know how you feel about me. Perhaps not entirely friendly? I will wait for you this coming Saturday in the café on your corner at about nine. I have something to say to you. I have a small request for you. It's a matter of my conscience. In case you don't remember me, I'm your sister Ariadna's friend, Sergei Samoilov.'

I read the letter ten times over, and from it I realised two essential things: first, that Ariadna was no longer with him; and second, that he had been in Paris for a long time but had never given me a thought until now.

Samoilov's letter in my hand, I left the kitchen, went to my room and sat there in the dark and cold for a long time. I was amazed that I had felt no presentiment. You would have expected a hard frost and pitch blackness, famine, terror, matches that didn't light and grass growing in the streets come spring. Who could turn up to complete a picture like that if not he? But the letter was a total surprise.

I turned on the radio very softly and spun the dial without seeing. Suddenly someone said gently and with all the conviction the human voice is capable of, 'You're still here? You're still here? But I swear to you, they're waiting for you. Everything's all set for your arrival. The orange trees are blooming in the gardens, and from the windows of the white villa you can see to the bottom of the sea. And you know, in the evening dark blue dragon-flies like you've never seen flit around the garden. It's time for you to go. It's time!'

A moment's silence. The thunder of applause. And, apparently, the heavy rustle of a falling curtain.

He had seen me two years before, but until now he hadn't given me a single thought.

But why should he think of me? Why should he remember that his wild, slender, bright-eyed lover had any relatives – a crazy father who had been adamantly opposed to him, and the boy or girl sibling of uncertain age whom Ariadna herself had abandoned so easily, whose letters she didn't answer and who had never played any role in her life.

They were people of another world, and they doubtless would have been stunned had they learned that Ariadna became a minor actress, at first acting in minor but avant-garde foreign dramas and later in home-grown political plays. Together the two had knocked around the theatres, first in Petersburg and later in the Crimea. She kept aiming for the Tairov, but there was never an opening for them in Moscow, and for several years they lived in Simferopol, where they acted until Ariadna contracted typhoid fever and died. Then (that was in 1928) he moved in with his sister in Tver, where he was arrested in some factory incident which his sister's husband had been mixed up in. He served a short prison term, four months altogether, and there was even a trial, after which he was sent to a camp on the White Sea Canal. There he met real political exiles, sectarians for the most part – Anabaptists, Old Believers and Seventh Day Adventists. And finally – through the snow, forests, a virgin Karelian birch grove, past a lake of such beauty and calm that he knew he had to go back some day, past border guards – from a distance, when they were buried in the snowdrifts, their helmets looked like dogs' heads and their bent sabres stuck out from under their greatcoats like tails – past all that, from snowdrift to snowdrift, carrying a hunk of stolen bread under his shirt, until he reached a hut that stood on stilts and had whimsical lintels, vermilion shutters and blue smoke coming from its lacquered chimney, where a little flag popped in the wind – a Finnish police station. Did you think it was the toy house in the fairy tale where the gingerbread dwarf lived?

'Two years of Helsinki and five years of Berlin, first as a truck driver, then as a magician, then as a cab driver. I moved to Paris, but I won't stay here forever. No, no. I might leave very soon. There's nothing to keep me here. Where will I go? East. East, naturally. I don't like oceans or islands. I like firm ground. That's why I'm in such a hurry. That is, I could have before, but there wasn't this real ne . . . necess . . .'

Only at this point did I notice his way of speaking without finishing his words.

'I'll explain my reason presently. This is very important to me. This is a request . . . This . . .'

He encircled and gripped the little round table our beer was on.

He had been plain, pale-faced, red-nosed, and his smile had been bleak. He was exactly the same, and his intelligent, sparkling eyes still cut right through me.

But apart from that his outward appearance had taken on that Russian shabbiness I knew so well. It was a special shabbiness that began and ended with our life abroad. Like fate, it missed a few – the dandies and the hell-raisers – and absorbed all the others, with their shiny clothes, frayed cuffs, worn ties and dingy handkerchiefs. Despite the fact that Samoilov looked more like an actor or a messenger than a former officer who was now a machine operator at Renault, his shabbiness was no different from the shabbiness of Varvara's friends.

'I look at your sweater,' I said, 'and it seems like the same one as before. Do you remember "The Tattered Cloak"?'

He shook his head. 'I never wore any cloak.'

'I'm not saying you wore one. You made it up. Remember, there was a part about Don Quixote and Lear?'

He looked attentively into my face, and suddenly something happened in his, something flared in his memory.

'That wasn't me, that was Zvonkov who thought that up. I had this comrade, he died in Siberia.'

'But no, that was you. I know. I'm sure. Have you really forgotten? It was an old-fashioned pelerine, and it was too far gone to mend.'

We both fell silent. I thought about Ariadna, about her translucent face, about her breasts, which glowed when she bathed in the tub. About that night she left us, tying the ribbons on her hood and taking a bundle on her arm, an age-old peasant-woman motion. And I thought about Samoilov, about the fact that he had lived two-thirds of his life and that this meeting held some special meaning for him. And also about how when he looked at me he didn't see me.

I never get upset, I'm generally very calm, but that evening I got terribly upset, as if something depended on this meeting, and my agitation interfered with my listening. I can recall the dim light of the lamp in the smelly café, the spots of dampness along the walls, and Samoilov, of course, who turned out to be shorter than I had thought. In my childhood he had seemed tall.

'I called you here on what is for me a very important matter, Alexandra Evgenievna,' he said, and he smiled at me in a new way, with his whole mouth. 'I would like to ask your father's forgiveness. The kind of forgiveness that is given when people repent. Could you help me do that?'

My face must have registered astonishment.

'I've sinned against him, sinned greatly. I took his daughter away from him. It was worse than stealing. I nearly killed him. The longer I put it off the more it torments me.'

Then I laughed right in his face.

'Do you really believe that nonsense? You must be out of your mind! Are there really people who believe that nonsense?'

He let go of the table, which he had been clutching all that time.

'I don't know what to say to that. Perhaps I'd do better to say nothing. Or to say that yes, there are people like that, who believe. You're foolish to imagine they don't. You know yourself that there are quite a few of them.'

I reached for the old, worn-out cigarette case from which he had just taken a cigarette.

'It's amazing,' I said, raising and lowering my shoulders, 'amazing, Sergei Sergeevich, that you think about things like that and talk about things like that. And you want to repent. Only my father – '

But he cut in. 'In the North, in the camp, I met people like that . . . I could tell you – '

A disturbance broke out in the small café where we were sitting. They were looking for someone's umbrella. We too had to get up. The waiter crawled under the benches on his hands and knees. A shaggy dog dozing by the extinguished stove started growling and opened his purulent eyes, and the curtain over the door (a torn billiard cloth) fluttered without letting the lavender light of the lamps escape when someone went in or out. It reeked of cheap red wine, as do all little Paris cafés, and your feet scuffled softly over the wet sawdust on the unswept floor. Wherever you looked your eye fell on wet rags, which from time to time that same waiter used to mop up puddles that had formed in the corners.

Samoilov's hands were large and clean, and he wore a slim wedding band on his skinny ring finger. I thought, Where did that ring come from? And just what does he do?

After a pause he suddenly asked, 'Am I keeping you? You must be busy. Couldn't I see your father? I want, I have to ask his for –'

'My father is dead.'

He remained seated, frozen. At that moment I realised that one could never find out what he was thinking, what he was feeling, from his eyes – his vivid, intelligent eyes.

'What do you know,' he said slowly, softly. 'In that case, forgive me for disturbing you needlessly.'

That was all. He put down a stack of change for the beer that he and I had drunk. Our handshake was firm and brief, and after that he turned left and I right. And it was so dark that no one could have seen my face.

The kitchen that night was full of smoke and fumes because Varvara was frying pancakes. Petrov, von Moor and Vasya Vostronosov, who was back from Brittany on leave (he had a scar over half his face, and still remembered General Wrangel), were sitting there and were already on their third each. I sat down with them immediately, crowding in. I had a drink and was soon laughing at how von Moor wrapped his pancake on his fork. And when I laughed like that, I could tell that my laugh was beginning to sound like a cry – the very image of Papa's and Varvara's. It runs in the family. And the vague feeling that I was powerless to do anything about my life made me laugh even louder. But it was better to laugh like that, with everyone around, than to cry alone into a stiff pillow, under a thin, striped blanket, in a room that was unheated all winter. After all, this was my life.

Our possessions are becoming more and more fragile. Each is the last; there won't be another. People grow transparent, and when they leave I have the feeling that they are just about to come back. Everything is disappearing: bread, paper, soap, thread, kerosene. The world is going to hell, but among it all a blessed light is burning quietly for me – not from the star, which went out a long time ago, but from a new source, like a fog filled with the trembling light of stars.

I can't explain when or how it came back. I no longer have my old ability to perceive with the unerring perspicacity of a child, the flair I once had. But I know that in our gloomy life, as I get duller and weaker, I am picking it up once again with special strength, special fervour. What it is that is being revived in the face of everything inside me (as it was twenty years ago) might – very approximately and clumsily – be called a search for grandeur, a thirst for wisdom, love and truth, although all those words are just part of one infinite thing that I seem to skirt without actually seeing. What kind of grandeur could visit a life of such poverty and vulgarity? What kind of wisdom is there in my work at the laundry or in my evenings spent in my aunt's kitchen? Where in my life is love, which has never touched me? And can I really be affected by truth, to which I never gave a moment's thought? Like twenty years ago, though, the sterile receptivity of my soul is becoming keener, as it is destined to be perhaps twice or three times altogether in a human life. And involuntarily I begin to think that one day, maybe in 1960, I will be faced again with an experience that is something like it.

But where will Samoilov be then, and how exactly will he give me the signal?

The Black Pestilence

I

The earrings had been at the municipal pawnshop for nine years. Much had happened in the world, events had taken place which had dazzled and shaken mankind. But the earrings remained in their numbered box, and for nine years I had paid interest on them. When your money is in the bank, everyone knows that it isn't actually there but circulating in the capitalist stream, returning as the need arises. But earrings, old clothes, gramophones and silver spoons lie there while you pay interest, and later, should you stop paying it, they slip away forever.

The municipal pawnshop in Paris is one of the most repugnant places I know. It stinks of disinfectant, the walls are painted grey, there are two rows of benches. Everyone knows why people come there. The clerk in the grey jacket takes the item, gives it a number, carries it away and a few minutes later calls out:

'Twenty-three! Seven hundred.'

That means they are giving you seven hundred francs for whatever it is you've brought. You walk up to the window and collect your money, unless the sum is too small, and then you ask them to give you back your property and you go away. There's nowhere else to go, though.

Sometimes when you pawn a valuable you can ask them to go up a little, but here only gold, platinum and diamonds are considered precious. Rubies, emeralds and sapphires are described as coloured stones and they fetch next to nothing. Pearls fetch nothing at all — they have a way of dying when separated from their owner.

Side by side on the long benches people sit awaiting sentence. Nine years ago I sat there too, between a woman who had brought four old sheets, and got nothing for them, and a man with a beard who looked like Lenin. He had brought some ancient book, and they offered him two hundred francs for it. He tried to explain that it was a 1747 edition, but the shout rang out:

'Yes or no?'

And he said, 'Yes.'

For the earrings, as I had expected, they gave me a wad of money. Each held a diamond the size of a small button, and both were of the purest white. Usually the municipal pawnshop gives one-third of the value, and I thought, yes, that's right, how many times did she tell me that if the earrings were sold, two people could live on them for half a year or so; that meant that by myself I could live on them for an entire year.

The money was spent that very day to pay the bills for her hospital and funeral. Only one bill was left unpaid: the last two blood transfusions. I had to sell her little gold watch. The jeweller who bought it told me to come back in a week.

'If I sell the watch for a good price,' he said, 'you'll get a little more.'

When I came back a week later, he said, 'I owe you another ten per cent. I sold the watch yesterday, and well. I never make more than twenty per cent. That's my rule.'

I thanked him.

'I like rules,' he added, with an embarrassed smile. 'Some people find them tiresome. But I think to live without rules would be venal.'

That was nine years ago. During that time I never had the money to redeem the earrings. And now I had decided to leave, to go to America. I'm not a particularly decisive character, but I told myself, the time has come, you can't go on living like this. My visa had arrived a week before and my place on the boat had already been reserved. I now needed money for the ticket and for the first months of my new life. The solution was to sell the earrings. Every sum had been carefully calculated; I don't like sitting around in the evenings with a pencil in my hand, doing calculations, but I know that everyone does, so I did too. That arithmetic was a small part of a great truth: know thyself.

In order to sell the earrings I had to redeem them. As for redeeming them myself, that was out of the question. So I went back to the jeweller.

He examined the pawnshop ticket closely.

'Yes, I've handled this kind of thing before,' he said, 'and I'll redeem your earrings tomorrow morning. Usually they give one-third the value. It looks like these could be sold for good money. Come by tomorrow, at midday.'

I arrived the next day. There was no one in the shop, but behind the curtain that separated the store from the workshop I could sense a presence. I coughed and began to inspect the rings and brooches under the glass; the whole shop ticked away with clocks, large and small.

He came out, holding open a velvet case lined in white satin.

'I have some bad news for you,' he said. 'If I'd known, I wouldn't have bothered. One stone is worthless. It has the black pestilence. Here, you can see for yourself.'

He put a large glass lens against my eye and I bent over the case. And as I looked at the stone, which was completely black, the earth seemed to cave in beneath my feet; a chasm was opening up and I was flying headlong into it, buildings were crashing down around me, San Francisco, Messina, Lisbon – earthquake scenes from old films which had somehow stuck in my memory.

'This couldn't have happened in nine years. This takes a million years,' said the jeweller, and there was something mournful in his voice, in his grey head tilted to one side. 'I don't understand how they could have made such a mistake. They never make mistakes. They have an expert there. Possibly he looked at the good stone and not at the other. You'd do well if you managed to get the same money that they were pawned for. To reimburse me. I can't sell these earrings.'

'You can't? But who can?'

'That's going to take some thinking. You're in big trouble.'

'When do you need your money back?'

He looked at me over his glasses.

'Put yourself in my position,' he said in his even voice. 'I redeemed your item, I took a sum of money out of my pocket. I would like to have it by this evening. As a matter of fact, I'm taking a risk – you might not come back at all.'

He brought me the telephone book and I started to search through it for the addresses of the jewellers he recommended.

'Sell them to whoever offers you the most,' he said. 'There's Oginson. Sometimes he gives a good price.'

'Oginson . . . O . . .' I began to flip through the book, forward and back. Everything in my mind was getting hazy. 'How odd, N comes right after M. There's no O for some reason.'

'O comes after N,' he said patiently.

'O comes after N,' I muttered. 'There's no O in this book at all. Obviously the pages must have been torn out.'

'That's impossible,' he said. 'O was always there.'

'Does it come before or after P?'

'Look right after N!' he shouted, suddenly afraid.

I found Oginson. We both calmed down.

'You know what else I would do if I were

you?' he said. 'I would go back to the pawnshop and try to pawn them for the original price, if they'll give it.'

I thanked him for his advice, and put the glass lens in my eye one more time. Millions of years. A black pestilence. The stone sat fast in its gold prongs.

'I hope,' said the jeweller, 'that you don't suspect me of switching your stone?'

'No,' I replied. 'That hadn't occurred to me.'

'That would be venal.' He walked to the corner of the room. 'I have rules.'

'I swear to you the thought hadn't crossed my mind!'

'I believe you. And they couldn't have done it at the pawnshop. They seal the box immediately, no one can get to it.'

We looked at each other.

'You know,' he said, 'sometimes in life there's a fact with no explanation, a question with no answer. It's rare, but it happens. Once I was sitting in my room and a letter disappeared from my desk. It was worth a lot of money. It was never found. No one could have taken it, no one came in. But it vanished. Yes, the more I think about it, the more I'm convinced that their expert had to have looked at the other stone.'

Messina and Lisbon, I thought, and the vanishing letter O, and it was all a nightmare. Just that morning everything had seemed so simple, and now the journey seemed inconceivable. But there was no time to lose. I wrapped the case up in my handkerchief.

'Don't lose it,' said the jeweller. 'And please, bring the money today.'

I went back to the pawnshop. There was a crowd of people in the squalid place. They gave me a number – 604 – and I sat down, between a woman with an old blanket on her knees, which had clearly been given back to her, and who was evidently at a loss for what to do now, and a very smartly dressed older man who looked like Nicholas the Second. I saw that he had brought a tortoise-shell fan. I can't think of any place in the world that is more vile, I thought.

'604!' they shouted from the window.

This time they had looked at both stones and the sum offered was half the original.

'This is a misunderstanding,' I said, upset. 'These earrings were redeemed this morning. You had given much more for them.'

The man in the grey jacket looked at me for a second, went behind the partition, and came back with the case.

'You're getting money for one stone,' he said, and I saw that he had a cataract in one eye. 'The other's worthless. You can take it back.' It was just like his eyes; one was completely worthless.

I passed through halls, up and down stairs, across courtyards. I saw five or six jewellers that day. No one would give me anything for the second earring, and they wouldn't give me enough for the first to allow me to pay off my debt. It was almost six o'clock when I finally reached Oginson's. It was a private apartment, not a shop, and a woman opened the door, which was on a chain.

'Who are you?'

I didn't know what to say.

'Who sent you?'

I explained. She went away, her slippers scuffing. A long time passed. Finally, the door opened and I was led down a long, dark passageway into a long, dark study. A fat man sat motionless behind a perfectly bare, smoothly polished desk. Two canaries chirped in their cage by the window, directly over his head.

He was fat, pale and old, immobile, and throughout our conversation he was reflected like a block of marble in the smooth surface of that vast bare desk.

'How much do you want?' he asked, having examined the stones, moving only his wrists. I named the figure I owed. He focused on some point beyond me.

'You'd have a hard time getting that much for one stone, and then only if it were remade into a ring,' he said. 'I don't need the other one.'

A silence ensued. The canaries shook their cage. The noise of the street filtered through the closed windows. There was a smell of dust and tobacco. I was trembling inside.

He examined the earrings once more.

'This pestilence,' he said slowly, 'has been in it from the very beginning. Before man even existed, this plague was already in it.'

I took a breath.

'But I'll give you your price. And I've changed my mind. I'll take the second stone, too.'

He took his wallet out of his pocket and counted out the money. I said a loud 'Good-bye!' as I walked out, but he didn't answer. On the street I stood for a moment, in shock: both Messina and Lisbon had rolled over me but I was still alive. I dropped off the money, returned home, hungry and tired, and collapsed on the bed and lay absolutely still until it was dark. If someone had given me a bomb that evening and said, throw it at whomever you want, I would have thrown it at . . . who would I have thrown it at? The first jeweller? The second jeweller? The man in the grey jacket? Mr Oginson? The municipal pawn-shop's expert? No, I told myself. I would have thrown it at that horrible hall which reeks of disinfectant, I would have thrown it at the entrance, at the sign: *Liberté*, *Egalité*, *Fraternité*. But as my fellow lodger, a man without profession, Michel Néron, says, Russians always manage to land on their feet, however tricky the circumstances. Russians are just plain lucky.

'Lucky at what?' I cried out later that night when he dropped by. 'How? At what?'

But he, of course, didn't know what to say; and as he couldn't bear shouting, he shrugged his shoulders, walked out without a word and went to his room.

The next day was Saturday, and when Sunday came I had time to think through what I should do. If I tried to sell all the things that belonged to me, instead of giving them away, I would only be able to get together about a quarter of what I needed to pay for the ticket. That much was clear without doing any calculations. Where was I to get the rest? In my mind, I ran through my possessions. Even if I were to sell everything, leaving just the clothes on my back, my razor and my toothbrush, it wouldn't be enough. There was no solution. I even started to consider going tomorrow morning to cancel my boat ticket. There wasn't anyone to borrow that kind of money from either. To write to Druzhin in Chicago would have been absolutely pointless, for one very simple reason which I won't mention now.

'There are two engagement rings,' I counted, 'and books, and clothes and a radio, old, but still good.' The day stretched on and on and I had to come to some kind of decision. In fact it seemed at moments as if everything had already been decided, and that there was nothing left to do, except to stop thinking about it.

Between five and six o'clock the hall clerk knocked at my door. 'Someone's asking for you downstairs,' he said. 'Some young lady.'

I smoothed my hair, put on a jacket and went down, feeling no curiosity at all. A young woman I didn't know was waiting for me on the lower landing. She was wearing trousers and had a cigarette in her mouth. There was no one around. A radio was wailing somewhere.

'How do you do,' she said in Russian,

extending her hand. 'My name is Alya Ivanova. May I come up?'

'How do you do,' I replied. 'My room is a
mess, forgive me. If you like, we can go up.'

Twice she glanced rapidly at me, and then
glanced once again as if my face were unusual
in some way, although my looks are rather
ordinary. When we walked into the room,
she looked around at the walls, the furniture,
and sat down on the only chair, by the
window. I sat down on the bed.

'I don't know how to explain all this to
you,' she said, looking at me with intense
black eyes. Her face was slender, with a tinge
of ill health, but you could see her energy and
strength in her hands. 'I found out that you're
going to America. Don't ask who told me.
There's a man who sells addresses. He knows
about everyone who's leaving. You go to
him, he takes out a sheet of paper, and there it
is, by *arrondissement*. That's for when you
want to rent a room.'

I replied quickly, 'What does this have to
do with me? Go and ask downstairs, ask the
landlady.'

She put out her cigarette.

'If I ask the landlady, she'll either give it to
whoever's next on her list, or else she'll give it
to me for a rent that's three times more than

yours. Your rent is cheap and they can't raise it. If I move in here with you and stay a month, the room would stay mine at the same rent. I could move in tomorrow morning.'

'But as you can see, there's only one bed here.'

'That doesn't matter. I can sleep on the couch.' In the corner, near the washstand, was a three-legged sofa, barely big enough for a child to sleep on.

'Haven't you ever heard of making money this way? According to the law, I have to live here with you for at least a month in order for the room to be mine. It will be awkward for you, I know, I'll be in your way, but what's to be done? I'll be paying you for it.'

I coughed.

'I'll pay you part of the money tomorrow, when I move in, and the rest, let's say, in two weeks. We're both taking a risk: you might kick me out; I might not pay you the last part. I've been told that some people bring in a third party, a witness; if you want I'm happy to do that. But in my opinion it's better to handle this sort of business without witnesses. Maybe we could do it all on trust?'

She fell silent but kept her eyes on me. Evidently she was waiting for me to say that you shouldn't do anything on trust.

I said, 'You paid to find out my address, and you're planning to pay me. Why, if you're rich, are you looking for a cheap room?'

'You're funny!' She smiled and I saw how pretty she looked with a smile. Her eyes shone even more brightly. 'I don't have a lot of money, but by giving you five thousand francs now, later I'll pay six hundred a month. At present I don't have my own place and I pay two thousand. Do you see?'

With five thousand francs, I could at least try and work something out, I thought.

'Right now I don't have my own place,' she repeated, and all of a sudden a shadow flitted across her face. 'I can't stay there any longer. I have to leave.'

I got up, walked around the room and sat down on the bed again. 'Let's talk about this as calmly as possible,' I said. 'Suppose I stay here for another month, which is more or less what I was planning to do. You would stay here, with me sleeping on the couch, of course, not you. We could also put the mattress on the floor, which would actually be even more comfortable. One without a mattress on the bed; the other on the mattress on the floor. When do you go out in the morning?'

'I don't.'

'Don't you work?'

'I work in the evenings.'

'Well, that works out even better. You would get in late, I'd already be asleep. In the morning I'd leave – and you'd be asleep.'

'Why are you so concerned about sleeping?' she asked. 'I've slept on the ground in summer camps since I was a child, in a sleeping bag, in a tent with everyone piled up together. I'm not worried about that at all. I thought you'd be more interested in putting it all down on paper. And I do want to say one thing: this is strictly an arrangement between you and me.'

'But you and I are making an illegal deal, so there's nothing to put down on paper.'

'Illegal? Pardon me, but there's nothing illegal about this deal. You're not passing me off as a sister, or as a wife. You're not deceiving anyone. We live together for a month, and then you leave – we aren't obliged to say that it's forever. I'll keep the room, and once a year passes after you leave, it will automatically transfer to my name.'

'Couldn't you move in just before I move out?'

'So that they could throw me out the next day?' She opened her purse and showed me a wad of notes.

'Here's two thousand, which you'll get tomorrow. I'll pay you the other two thousand in two weeks' time and one thousand just before you leave. That's how it's done, apparently.'

I stood up, walked over to her, and surprised myself by saying, 'I want the whole five thousand this week. I have to pay for my ticket. I can't wait.'

That didn't frighten her in the slightest; it even seemed to please her.

'Fine,' she said. 'So be it. I had no idea you were so greedy.' She smiled, looking at me fearlessly.

'Come on – if you have the time, let's have some coffee,' I said, unable to sit like that any longer looking at her. We went downstairs and out onto the street. By the door, on the pavement, stood the landlady, Madame Beauvaux, and as we walked past her Alya Ivanova calmly placed her hand on my shoulder, as is the custom with Parisian women, announcing to her and to the passers-by and to the whole city that I was her property, her captive.

We sat down at a table in a café and Alya, having barely sipped her coffee, went to make a phone call. The phone booth was three steps away from me, and I could hear fragments of the conversation: she was talking with someone called Zina and telling her that 'he' was asking for the entire amount by next week. She asked her to ask Jeannot what he thought, what she should do. Then, evidently in answer to a question, she replied, 'No, he's clearly honest. Absolutely! But he insists.'

We sat for half an hour. She smoked, thoughtfully and quietly. I looked at her: her body seemed very long, as if she had been stretched. Her hair was smooth and short, her ears narrow, her face an even oval and her neck a little bit too long. Her complexion, very pale, was exceptionally pure and clear, and her whole being gave the impression of clarity; there was never a trace of hidden meaning, ambiguity or enigma in her eyes or in her smile. That impression came, no doubt, from her clear black eyes, from the way she looked at things around her and, occasionally, at me.

My conscience was anything but easy, though. I felt embarrassed at the thought of taking her money. The month I faced living with her in a single room first seemed wretchedly inconvenient in the simplest everyday sense – no sleep, no privacy, constantly feeling cramped and inhibited – and then seemed suddenly easy, silly even. In any case, it would be unlike anything else I'd experienced.

She moved in the following day. She had one suitcase, old, black and tattered. In order not to embarrass me, the only thing she took out was a flashy theatrical costume – a wide, raspberry-coloured tulle skirt with a sequinned bodice. It had to be hung on the door, on the hook, and nearly filled the room. Together we dragged the mattress onto the floor and each of us made our own bed (she had brought two sheets and a small pillow), after which she washed up, changed her clothes, pencilled her eyes and dressed in that raspberry skirt, trying not to crush it, sat down on the edge of the chair and told me that she danced at the Empire, that she had two numbers in the show, that she had been working with a partner for four years already and at one time they'd even appeared in the Casino de Paris. Ten years before, while still in her teens, she had studied with Olga Osipovna and had thought she would be a ballerina, but fate had decided differently.

'Who's your partner?' I asked.

'My partner broke my finger three months ago, but I can't get rid of him; they'd fire us both. We're no use without each other.'

'Did he break it on purpose or by accident?'

'On purpose, of course, and it was during a performance! He didn't like something, he's so nervous and touchy. He grabbed me after catching me in a leap and broke my little finger out of spite. I was in hospital three days after that. They wanted to operate, but I got by.' She extended the little finger on her left hand and examined it closely.

'Crooked?'

'No, I don't think so.'

'Well, I think so,' she said, and she frowned. The corners of her mouth drooped, but a minute later she was smiling at me.

'I'll leave the costume at the Empire, I'll set it up, otherwise it's going to clutter up your room. Nice costume? You like it? Goncharova designed it for me.'

When she had gone and I was left alone, a thousand thoughts assailed me. The sensation of humiliation, impotence, of all my human worthlessness and weakness gripped me. I felt – for the umpteenth time – my disgraceful inability to wake myself up, to regenerate, to live like other people. What would Druzhin say if he knew? It was a pity that I couldn't write to him about it! Then I considered everything from the perspective of Michel Néron, from the standpoint of a sober and sensible man. Yesterday a fine precious stone was switched on me for a bad one, and today someone moved into my room. Yesterday I made no attempt to complain, and today I didn't drive her out. Some people are like steel springs, as resilient as tennis balls. It was quite clear that Alya wasn't going to pay me anything, and that the whole deal with Oginson had been fixed up beforehand.

But that only lasted for one moment, and then my thoughts took a new tack: the old wooden screens that closed off the washstand and the stool with the spirit lamp, the skillet and the tea kettle were going to play a leading role in our future life together. They were easy to move and set up, to shift this way and that; but as the first few days showed, I was the only one who had any need of screens. Alya didn't need them at all: accustomed in theatres to dressing and undressing wherever and in front of whomever she had to, she shed her clothing calmly and without a hint of embarrassment, down to her little black knickers and narrow black brassière, and went to wash herself. And her body, on which each muscle was developed and which fed her by its artistry, was just like her face: pure, clear, and yet slightly incorporeal.

On the Wednesday morning she gave me the money and I paid for my ticket. The two engagement rings made up the balance. By the end of the first week our life together had already taken on a reassuringly routine aspect; the only thing which preoccupied me was the thought of having taken money for something that, in essence, did not belong to me. I got up in the morning at seven o'clock while Alya slept soundly, her face to the wall; at eight I left (at the time I was working for an architect, selecting coloured tiles for mosaics and sometimes I even did sketches for those mosaics, which earned me the title of 'artist'). I got back at eight-thirty in the evening, having put in overtime, since the work was there. When I came in, having eaten already, Alya usually wasn't there. Everything in the room had been carefully tidied, the mattress had been pushed under the bed, a glass of anemones stood on the table and her beads hung from a nail by the window. The coffee pot was full of coffee, which I heated up and drank; I went to bed at twelve o'clock, and had usually dozed off before her return. She came in at about one and turned on the table lamp, immediately blocking off the light.

About ten days before my departure, I woke up in the night and saw her sitting in her old robe at the table, eating a chocolate bar and some bread and reading a book. The lamp was shaded with something dark blue. The blue light fell on her bare leg, on her long, extended, pale instep. She couldn't tear herself away from the book. And her profile, bent so attentively over the page, her tiny black head, the sight of her long gaunt hand raking her hair, for some reason suddenly made my heart ache; I experienced a strange happiness from the fact that she was there, and so close to me.

'Time to sleep,' I said softly.

She started, removed her hand, smiled. 'How are you doing down there on the floor? Can't you sleep?'

'I'm fine. I love it on the floor. But what do you care about me? Why do you ask?'

Still smiling, she continued to read, and I shut my eyes and began listening to the sounds that reached me: the occasional scraping of her chair; the pages of her book being turned; her chocolate bar between her teeth; and little by little, in that harmony of sounds that oscillated around me, I began to fall asleep. Only one thought, somewhere deep down in my conscience, poisoned my happiness: her money.

A few days later, as I was leaving the office

during lunch, I ran into Barrister N., whom I hadn't seen for a long time. We were both delighted.

'Fate has sent you to me,' I told him. 'You know, only yesterday I was thinking about you. I wanted to stop by for some advice.'

We went to get some lunch together, and I let him talk about himself. He complained about some relatives of his wife with whom he had some tangled financial relations. Then, having exhausted that theme, he asked me about my 'case'.

'Or better yet, maybe we should go back to my office?'

It turned out to be quite close by, and there, to the constant ringing of telephones, I told him about Alya and asked him whether they would evict her from my room or let her stay after I left.

'They have to let her stay,' he said. 'She's absolutely right. Good for her. No one can kick her out, nor can they raise the rent. She's been clever. And you, my dear friend, have been had. I could have found you a much better customer. Why didn't you come to me?'

'I had no idea. And you don't think it was dishonourable on my part to take her money?'

'Dishonourable? What a word! Everyone

does that nowadays. You'd simply be a fool if you let a chance like that slip. And she was lucky. Incredibly lucky. You can't imagine the things that happen. Right now I've got a case coming to trial: the person didn't move out. A month passed, another, a third, and the two of them are still living there. I tell her (in this case she was supposed to have left and he to have stayed), I tell her, Madame, you gave your word (in addition to her word, of course, I had seen both her passport and her ticket), and now you sit there as if you were pinned down. You took the money but you haven't gone anywhere! And she says to me, Where am I supposed to go? I like it here, I've got no place to go, we're getting along fine. That's what she thinks, but he's taking her to court. Quite possibly my mother-in-law thinks we're getting along fine, too.'

Then came the last Sunday. On Sundays Alya had matinées, so she left at one o'clock, came back at four, and at eight went out again. On Sunday we always had dinner together. I waited for her and we set out for the restaurant on the corner, where we had 'our' little table. A fat waitress brought us our food while humming a tune, and an accordion player came, a grey-haired Hungarian, and played, seated on a stool the proprietor brought out for him.

'Alya,' I said, 'this is our last Sunday. I sail on Thursday. Are you satisfied?'

The question amazed her.

'Satisfied?' she echoed. 'I can't answer that. Yes, this is what I wanted when I came to see you. But on the other hand, I've grown rather close to you. It's been very cosy, even if the room's small. Maybe you'll reconsider and stay?'

I was so surprised that words failed me.

'Don't stay,' she continued, and even sighed. 'Your Druzhin is waiting for you there. Even his name says so – from *druzhba*, "friendship".'

I looked at her and said, trying to pretend that what I said should not be taken entirely seriously, 'He's been waiting a long time, he can wait a little longer. I warn you, Alya, I'm going to send you back all the money you gave me. It will be easy, as soon as I start working, in four months, maybe even in three. That money has been on my mind night and day, and I can't go on like this. I'll send it to you as soon as I can.'

The joke didn't come across, and she replied solemnly, 'You don't owe me anything, Evgenii Petrovich. There's no point in your worrying about that. Before, I was renting a fine, big room, but it was beyond my means. And they had four children in the apartment and the whole situation was very hard.'

'Noisy?'

'Not noisy. I just felt sorry for them. The father and mother were getting a divorce and the children were on their own all day long. No one taught them, and how they wanted to learn! The oldest boy was already twelve, and the girl ten. They literally swallowed whole everything I told them, and what do I know? When I studied with Olga Osipovna, I never had any time to read a book, and then I had to make money, to struggle, and I was in no mood for reading. I'm completely uneducated, I know absolutely nothing, but those children simply clung to me, they wanted to know everything, and there was not a single book in the whole house. I used to cry over it. They had never been to school and their parents didn't care. All day long they talked with each other – they didn't have any toys, not even little ones – they did nothing but discuss things: Why this? Why that? And do you know what I did? I reported them to the police. And then I had to leave.'

'Who did you report?'

'The parents. You know, there's a law that parents are required to send their children to school. Otherwise there's a fine and they force them to send the children. So I went to the police station and reported them. At first I wanted to send an anonymous letter to the police chief, but then I decided, I have to be brave, I'll go myself. I said, all four of them are exceptional, they never fight or break anything. They teach each other arithmetic on their fingers, they've worked out their own system, and all they do for hours on end is ask, Why is there thunder? Why are there stars? What's beyond the stars? How many years do dogs live? Who was Napoleon? Do something to help, I said. So the police chief thanked me and, can you imagine, they did everything they were supposed to, and not long ago three of them started school and the fourth is in kindergarten, and all four are at the head of their class. How happy they must be!'

I didn't say anything.

'Do you think it was bad to report them to the police?' she asked, frowning.

I still said nothing. Finally I said the first thing that came into my head.

'If someone gave me a bomb and said, throw it at anyone you like, I would blow up the entire planet.'

'Who would give you a bomb, Evgenii Petrovich?' she said, very seriously. 'And what kind of a bomb would it have to be, anyway, to blow up the planet?'

Four days later I left. Alya came to see me off at the station. I told the landlady, my girlfriend is staying, but I'm going. She winked (she had a habit of winking, it must have been a tic) and replied, 'It doesn't matter to me who lives there, just as long as they pay.'

'Ah,' I said, 'in that respect she's even better than I am: the first of the month is sacred to her.' We shook hands.

When the train left and Alya waved her handkerchief at me, I thought I saw something unfamiliar cross her face, something I had never seen in it, a flash of sadness, and seriousness, and a clouding of her clarity – I don't know the words to describe it. So much happens in life that has no description, no name. So many questions are left, in the end, without answers (for example, is it all right to report people to the police?). There are so many things that cannot be explained. The pestilence that I've had inside me for the last million years . . .

Michel Néron came to the station, too. He wasn't interested in Alya; he had two girlfriends of his own. He waved his handkerchief

97

as well. And for a little while my two friends, the two witnesses to my lonely Paris life, kept even with the window I was leaning out of and told me, 'Write, Zhenya, write to us about how it's going. And help us to get out of here. Don't be selfish, do you hear?'

II

Sometimes in May, after two or three warm summery days, the weather suddenly turns cold and rainy. The trees, like the birds who have only just returned to their nests, see time standing still, if not going backwards. The leaves, which have barely emerged, do not unfurl but wait, like the tips of little brushes. The bird, having chirped timidly earlier in the day, now cowers under a ledge, waiting for the bad weather to pass. Outside the rain falls without cease for a whole week, the sky rests on the house, the wind carries clouds, it's cold. And passers-by on the street smell of camphor and naphthalene, having once again taken out the warm waistcoats, jackets and coats that had been laid away for the following autumn.

The smell of camphor and naphthalene, as everyone knows, is death to love. Perhaps some of the mothballs, some of the moth crystals don't get cleaned out of the cuffs, perhaps people pull their warm things out of cupboards so hastily that they don't turn out all the pockets. Here and there on the streets there's a whiff of naphthalene, and houses smell of camphor. And since both of them are death to love, no one that May (which seems more like November) thinks of love, no one understands love, and there are even some who are not far from condemning it, either in themselves or in other people.

But Lev Lvovich Kalyagin had not felt the effects of the weather for a long time: he hardly ever left the house, and never looked out of the window. In his house, winter and summer, the temperature was always the same, controlled automatically; the light was always the same, and only when he went outside – very rarely and with much trepidation – did he inquire as to the month, the day of the week and the temperature – Celsius and Fahrenheit.

I worked for him for about a year. I did not find him immediately upon arriving in New

York. For a whole month I shuttled around town, looking for work. The last of Alya's money was running out and my hotel presented me with a bill that I couldn't pay. It was then that I saw an advertisement in the paper: 'Secretary wanted'.

He received me standing at first, but towards the end of our interview he sat down and indicated an armchair to me with his rubber-tipped cane.

He had the gaze of an eagle and a quavering voice. He said, 'Your duties, Arsenii Petrovich . . . '

'Evgenii.'

' . . . will include typing my correspondence in two languages and keeping accurate track of my affairs. I have two litigations in progress, one here and one in Europe. My wife is living in Switzerland and I pay all her bills. I'm writing my memoirs. It is essential that my archives be sorted out, that everything is numbered and put into folders . . . My daughter lives with me but she has refused to help me. My situation, Arsenii Petrovich . . . '

'Evgenii.'

' . . . is a difficult one. On the one hand, there is so much still to be done – I have an obligation to posterity. On the other, there's no way of knowing how much time I have left to do it in. That is, no one has any way of knowing – it's the secret of destiny!'

With a majestic sweep, he turned his hawk-like profile towards me. 'And now, if you're not in a hurry, I would like to ask you . . . ' Suddenly he made a strange sound, like a whimper. 'I'd like to ask you to iron a handkerchief for me, my favourite one. I washed it myself, but life never taught me how to iron. And Ludmila, my daughter, she's getting divorced, which does not suit her temperament.'

Somewhere in the apartment on the other side of the wall there was the sound of movement, a door slammed, and another, quick steps rang out, and a woman of about thirty-five walked into the room. She was short, with a hard but vaguely attractive face. She looked at us both and without saying anything but with an expression of profound contempt on her face, turned on her heels, walked out and slammed the door after her.

Kalyagin paid no attention whatsoever to the commotion.

'I'll tell you something else: I feel bad about troubling you, but I absolutely have to have a button sewn on. It's been three days' – again he whimpered – 'since I've been without that button. It's an embarrassment. But to thread a needle – no, when we were young we weren't taught that! I remember everything I was ever taught, but needling a thread . . . '

'Threading a needle.'

' . . . was not considered an appropriate subject.'

The door opposite opened quietly. Ludmila Lvovna poked her head in and said, 'Have you ever taught me anything?'

Kalyagin smiled guiltily. 'Allow me to introduce you. This is my daughter.'

'How do you do.' She walked in and stood in the middle of the room. I stood as well.

'Don't get up. I don't want to disturb you. I only want to say that you shouldn't believe everything that people tell you. Has he reached the part about "serving the Tsar" yet? No? Then you've still got lots of fun in store.'

'Don't pester us, please,' said Kalyagin, not in the least angry.

'One chapter of his memoirs is going to be called, "How I Wore a Red Ribbon in 1917".' Suddenly she looked me up and down. 'Of course, no one now will ever know whether that's true or false.'

She walked out and slammed the door shut again. Kalyagin looked at me. 'You see,' he said, 'that's what she's like. Just like her mother.'

My job began that very day. First I sewed on his button, then I ironed his handkerchief, and later I sat down at the desk and began looking through his papers. His wife wrote to him often. Almost every letter included a request for money, and all of them began more or less like this: 'Yesterday Daisy and I read and reread your last letter. It hurts Daisy so much that you don't like her! Often she only has to hear your name and she starts to cry (you didn't even remember her birthday!). Poor thing, she has no one in the world but me. Once again we are forced to move from this hotel and find another. Write *poste restante*. No one wants us to stay on anywhere . . . ' Then there were business letters: a lawyer writing from London about interest-bearing securities; a letter from Geneva about selling some property. There were numerous letters from distant relatives all over the world: from Formosa, from the Canary Islands, from Persia – one asked for money to patent an invention, another for money for his son's education, yet another for money to go to Paris. And finally there was a file for the papers on the factories in which Kalyagin invested his capital. In a week I already knew all of it by heart. On my way out I sometimes had to put iodine on his waist; he believed that iodine was a universal panacea. His body was well groomed, a touch yellow, with large birthmarks.

After four months I sent the money I owed her to Alya in Paris, and I felt the time had come to start saving for the move to Chicago. I thought of Druzhin. I kept a clear picture of him in my mind at all times; you could say that I never let him out of my sight. In the evenings I thought about him, and sometimes I felt a need to tell someone about him.

At first I didn't see Ludmila Lvovna at all. She lived on the upper floor of the apartment, where I never ventured. In the mornings an old Irishwoman came in to wash the dishes from the previous evening, straighten the rooms and prepare dinner. Kalyagin had dinner at midday alone, in the big dining room; the maid served him, cleared and left. She must have thought he was deaf, because from the study I often heard her shouting at him.

'Your supper is in the icebox. You only have to heat it up. Heat the blue pot on the stove and pour the contents into the white bowl, then pour what's in the glass cup over it all. All right?'

Kalyagin answered, 'All right. I'm not deaf.'

'I shout so that you don't do it backwards. Then there's stewed fruit for you. Old people shouldn't eat raw fruit. The doctor said you don't have enough fauna in your intestines.'

'I hear you.'

'Goodbye.'

In the early days I would go out, eat a sandwich, drink some coffee. Later Kalyagin said I should have dinner with him, and then in the evening, before going, I usually poured what was in the blue pot into the white bowl – or vice versa, which pleased him greatly.

It was six months after I'd come to the Kalyagins that I had my first conversation with Ludmila Lvovna. That day Lev Lvovich had gone out to a formal dinner with his old classmates (or perhaps they were from his regiment, I can't remember exactly). I spent an hour or two with him while he prepared himself, put him finally in a taxi and, going back, went into his bedroom intending to put his closet and dresser drawers in order. He had been asking me to do that for a long time.

She walked in wearing hat and gloves and sat down by the door, on a chair. Her face was dry, and her eyes had that hardness I had already noticed. In a sharp, mocking voice she said, 'You can tell right away: European. No American would let himself go from being a secretary to a cook, then a launderer, then a servant.'

'If you think that I'd be insulted by that, then you're wrong. I'm docile by nature, and I'm not bothered about being a cook or a servant.' My reply surprised her, and she said nothing for a few moments. I folded Kalyagin's shirts neatly.

'How much is he paying you?'

'Excuse me,' I said, 'but that's between us. It's none of your business.'

She narrowed her eyes. 'You don't realise who you're dealing with,' she said, and shook the tip of her foot. 'My parents are both mad, lonely and unhappy. They made me mad, lonely and unhappy too. But they don't admit it and I do.'

I continued to open and shut the dresser drawers.

'They're living in a dream world. They're sleepwalkers,' she went on. 'And I lived like a sleepwalker until I realised that one day you're a sleepwalker and the next you're taken away. All their generation is sick and irresponsible. Look at what they've done to the world. And if you tell them to think it all through – who they are, what they've done with themselves, their lives, their children – they try to wriggle out of it as much as they can and then they cry.'

'But they aren't all as unhappy as that,' I replied, still uncertain as to how I should act with her, whether to keep up her conversation or stay out of it. 'Sometimes they're very happy and even, in their own way, happier than you or I.'

She opened her large handbag and the room suddenly smelled of perfume; she took out cigarettes and matches and lit up.

'But I absolutely do not consider happiness the most important thing in life. What counts is a sense of responsibility and logic. And they don't know the first thing about that! They don't know what they're doing. Maybe the Kingdom of Heaven will open up to them because of it, but personally I wouldn't encourage all those meek and simple people. They've already wrecked enough.'

'Pardon me,' I interrupted her, 'but you said that your parents are lonely, unhappy people. If I've understood it, your mother isn't lonely – she has a companion or a relative with her, doesn't she?'

'You mean Daisy?'

'Yes.'

Ludmila Lvovna looked at me coldly, 'That's her Pekinese.'

At that moment the phone rang and I went into the study. When I returned Ludmila Lvovna was already gone. The room smelled of perfume, and a cigarette butt smouldered in the ashtray. I stood there a few minutes, listened for a door shutting somewhere, but this time she had vanished without a sound.

Every evening, as I left for my hotel, I thought about how, despite my complete solitude in this city, I was no worse (and no better) off here than I'd been previously. From time to time, as I had for the last ten years, I would occasionally dream the dream that haunted me and had become one of the secret cornerstones of my life. It is almost impossible to relate it in words. Nothing happens in it. I move in a thick, yellowish fog, as if on wheels, without making a sound. The sensation of a scorched desert. The sensation of speechlessness and the absence of time. On my path I sometimes come across strange plants, grey, greyish-yellow, like everything that surrounds me, like me. Perhaps I've been swaddled? Or am I a wooden doll with inarticulate arms and legs? The plants are thorny, dry and mute, they are motionless. Slowly I glide between them. Ahead everything is just the same . . .

I told myself that my life here was temporary, that I had finally made an effort, a decision, a resolution, had surmounted various obstacles, exercised my will and, perhaps, found a way to slip out of my quasi-existence. Nevertheless, I was more and more convinced that I was merely a simple being, closer to A B C than to quantum theory.

Lev Lvovich also lay somewhere between those two poles. He was made up of several elements, one of them his attachment to a certain middle-aged lady, whom he never introduced to me but of whom he spoke more than once.

'There was a time when I was considered quite a connoisseur with regard to the female sex, the personification, so to speak, of the demand which engenders supply. Now I am abandoned by everybody and I sometimes feel a need to hold her warm hands in mine. My hands are always ice cold, it's very unpleasant, and I want to warm them up, I want to feel a live woman near to me. You understand me, of course. Passions, jealousies, romanticism, that's all over now, but the poor orphan needs a woman's protection.'

Whenever this need became urgent he asked me to put him through to her on the telephone. She had a long first name, a long

patronymic, and a long, double-barrelled sur-
name, and he would say tenderly into the
telephone, 'I miss my angel. I'm freezing, your
orphan is cold. Have pity on a helpless sufferer
who already has one foot in the grave.'

Another element were his two friends. The
first was called Pavel Pavlovich, and he belonged to that chapter in Kalyagin's memoirs
which Ludmila Lvovna referred to as 'serving
the Tsar'. The other was called Peter Petrovich, and he belonged to the next chapter,
which was referred to, once again in Ludmila's words, as 'How I Wore a Red Ribbon in
1917'.

The third element to Kalyagin was the Russian church. He went either with Pavel Pavlovich to one or with Peter Petrovich to another,
and sometimes, when he was too lazy to travel
very far, to yet a third, where they did something in a different way from the first two.
He returned from church, as he himself put it,
pacified, looking rather less hawkish. Once in
a moment of peace and, apparently, mercy, he
inquired whether I too, like certain others,
considered Stalin to be the Peter the Great of
our time.

For a split second I decided the hour had
come for us to go our separate ways, that it
was time to send him, his wife, his lawyers and

his memoirs to the devil, but five minutes later he had already forgotten his question – his memory was failing by the day – and never again did the subject of politics come up between us.

Two weeks after my first conversation with Ludmila Lvovna, I found a note from her on my desk: 'If you're free this evening, come up and see me.' I went up after six. She was wearing a light, pastel dress, sandals and a large pearl necklace, and although her face was as hard as ever, she smiled and played hostess, walking nimbly around the room, perching from time to time on the sofa and on the arm of a chair. I sat and thought how surprising it was that she and I should suddenly have so much to talk about. At the same time our silences, in which we would both camouflage ourselves now and then, quickly became easy, calm, delightful even.

Thinking back to that first evening, I try to find in it something that might have hinted at what was to follow, and I find it above all in the very fact of her inviting me upstairs. Why do that? Probably out of boredom and curiosity. I cannot believe that Ludmila's love for me – a love that was not returned, naturally – had begun before that point. I was impressed by her eyes: grey, with a blueness around the pupil, candid eyes, with a forthright gaze that she never took off me. We immediately began talking about people's faces, about how they had changed over the last twenty years, about what they had looked like a hundred years ago, and a thousand years ago. ('It may be that a thousand years ago they were more like us now than in Schiller's time,' she said.)

'Your face is rather unusual,' she remarked. 'I mean its shape, there's something about it that's not quite . . . I can't find the word.' And right then the expression on her own face softened; goodness and humour animated it.

'What do you mean! No one's ever said that to me before!' I exclaimed (which was the absolute truth) and accidentally knocked over my glass. Fortunately, it was nearly empty. Suddenly I felt that the time had come to start talking about Druzhin. 'I have a friend in Chicago. Now there's a face for you! You can't look at that face without laughing.'

The conversation did not, as one might expect, stop there, did not shift from the general to the specific and then turn to something else. No, we lingered there. I mentioned Druzhin and she wanted to find out who he was.

'To begin with,' I said, and suddenly I

knew that I was just about to make her laugh, 'to begin with, he doesn't realise it, but he bears an uncanny resemblance to a horse.' As I had foreseen, Ludmila Lvovna burst out laughing. 'And then, to tell you the truth, he has this theory: he only likes people who remind him of horses. He thinks they're nobler.'

'Doesn't he see himself?' she managed to say, through her laughter.

'No.'

'Where are those people?'

'He looks for them. At one time he dreamed of forming a secret society of horse faces.'

After prolonged laughter a silence fell over her, and we looked at one another for a few minutes without speaking. For some reason it seemed to me that it was precisely at that moment that a change began to take place in her. It was amazing how the outlines of her cheekbones and jaw softened, how her forthright gaze suddenly acquired a tenderness and flexibility, a luminosity even, and sadness. Her thin hands suddenly unfolded and I saw her beautiful fingers, which I had a great desire to squeeze, to intertwine together with mine and then press to my face. I didn't move.

I remember she started talking about herself. Her great-grandfather had spent his entire life in bed. That was how she put it: 'My great-grandfather spent his entire life in bed, and from time to time his serfs turned him over. On a Turkish sofa. My grandfather married three times: the first time to a Gubkina, the second to a Veryovkina and the third to a Stolovshchikova. The family business prospered, their factories spewed smoke all over Russia. My father . . . what did my father ever do? I don't think he ever did anything. And he found out that it was possible to live like that. Oh, my youth, my innocence! I got married six years ago, and now I'm in the process of getting a divorce. My husband left me, he said, "I don't understand what's happening, but living with you is impossible. You have absolutely no sense of humour. A woman has to have at least some sense of humour." I have no idea what that meant, do you?'

Music was playing on the radio. There was a stack of books on the table, of which I wanted to read each and every one and another next to it which had colour reproductions which I wanted to look through. I wanted to sit next to her, look through books, listen to the soft string quintet on the radio, watch her sweet-smelling hair all fall to one side of her tilted face. She was talking about how 'paradise' meant 'garden' in some language I didn't know, that she had read about it somewhere, and 'hell', probably, was a boring room in some government institution where people waited – you know, there are places like that in courts, pawn-shops, train stations . . . It seemed to me that I'd heard that too, about a big grey room painted in oil paint, with benches, where the windows are never opened, where it smells of disinfectant. I was sure that I had been there myself, that she was talking about something I knew well.

'That tired old legend – about how para-dise is deadly boring and hell is full of interesting people, all of whom you know – ought to be ditched. In paradise Socrates and Homer converse and anyone can listen in, and in hell there's nothing but tedious bureau-cracy and loathsome officials.'

'With a cataract in one eye,' I put in.

'With a cataract in one eye,' she echoed. 'And the hour hand doesn't budge for milli-ons of years.'

'Whereupon a tiny little window closes.'

'Whereupon a tiny little window closes and then there's absolutely nowhere to go. And in paradise . . . '

' . . . horses stand in clean stalls, dark bay, light bay, roan, black, dappled,' I slipped in.

' . . . dappled, and so clean that you want to rest your cheek against their smooth sides. And everyone has a face a little bit like yours . . . ' Suddenly she broke off, as if she somehow had frightened herself into silence.

'Why like mine?' I asked, surprised.

'I don't know,' she said shyly, and cut the conversation short.

She had never been to Chicago and she had only a vague impression of it, and although I had never been there either, I told her that once Druzhin had written to me about it.

'First of all, there are some places which have been created by Piranesi.'

'You don't say!'

'I assure you,' I continued, and my voice rang with the firmest conviction. 'It seems that there is a Piranesi at work there – not the famous one, the museum one, but a descendent, his double, closer to us, our contemporary. This one, ours, works in steel instead, the same steel that is used for bolts or rails, that has been in the forge at the same time as automobile parts, taking from them something that the other Piranesi, the museum one, never knew. You see it especially in those stormy gloomy neighbourhoods that run south from the northern reaches of the river, passing by several train stations, hugging the canal on two sides and getting lost between Goose Island and the wharfs. On those narrow streets, from roofs to pavements, there are staircases on the outside, fire escapes, like broken lines in the air, against a sky that is white in the day or red at night. Those stairs make you think of the reverse side of life, of buildings, of the city, they make you think of the flies backstage in a gigantic theatre. Once in a while motionless figures sleep on them, hunched and hanging like black sacks, and it's as though these sleeping people hadn't lain down on the steel by chance but had battled for their sleep in a brawl, or haggled for it in a drunken quarrel. Those gloomy neighbourhoods are part of the city, they are like veins running through the city – narrow in the north, where they struggle to reach the Gold Coast and creep nearly all the way to The Loop, and broad near the harbour and also where they head south towards the factories, the granaries and the slaughterhouses.'

'Have you ever been there?' she asked, looking at me in amazement.

'No, I haven't.'

'How do you know all that?'

I didn't answer.

'Tell me more.'

'I'll tell you about the river. It's a highly original river. At one time it passed under sixty bridges before emptying out into the lake, but now it's the other way around, it flows out of the lake and through canals and rivers to the Mississippi Valley. The water is so turgid and filthy that no one would ever drown themselves in it. On one bank there's a forbidding hulk of a prison; on the other, like ships emerging from the fog that comes in from the lake, stand the tallest buildings in the world. There's no particular logic: North Avenue runs from east to west. West Side runs from north to south. The southern part of town is called the East Side, and the sun, which rises from out of the water, also seems to set in the water; when it sets in the west, red reflections fall on the water to the east. Fogs travel north, sailing past a magnificent lake that's like the Mediterranean for this hemisphere, but at the same time it's also the great waterway "from the Varangians to the Greeks", that is, from the Gulf of St Lawrence to the Caribbean, and from Labrador to the West Indies, and the Chicago shore lies along this great waterway.'

'Did you make that up yourself?'

'I don't think so, no.'

At that moment the clock on the mantelpiece chimed softly, just as it does in the Moscow Arts Theatre during the third act of *A Month in the Country*. I jumped up. Had I already been here with her for four hours? We had talked for twenty minutes about heaven and hell and an hour and a half about Chicago. Even if one counted another half-hour for her story about her grandfather, that still didn't add up to four hours. Where had the time gone?

'Where has the time gone?' I exclaimed. 'Where?'

'I didn't take it, I swear I didn't take anything away from you. Don't shout like that. If someone heard you they'd think you were being robbed.'

'Forgive me. Now you will never invite me back again . . . '

She laughed. 'I think,' she said, 'your horse-faced Druzhin has written you some very extraordinary letters. Come again. Or have you already told me all you know?'

'Oh, no. I've got a lot more to tell.'

Now we both laughed, and I left. 'Where did she get a clock like that?' I thought on my way home. 'Probably an inheritance from her grandfather.'

I thought about her, and about her femininity which she hid as if it were something to be safeguarded in secret, not for everyone. It was being safeguarded, and now it was being shown to me, I thought. Why? What was I supposed to do with it?

A week later she and I were at a concert, in a new hall that had opened in a museum building, panelled in dark wood.

'It's like sitting inside a contrabassoon,' she said, laughing. She was high-spirited that evening, high-spirited and elegant, almost too elegant. People were looking at her and admiring her.

I took her home and went upstairs. She immediately switched on the radio and once again I heard the exact same music I had heard the first time, as if I had never left her at all.

'So how are things in Chicago?' she asked, settling into the corner of the sofa.

I slowly shifted my eyes from the radio to the clock, from the clock to her.

'People there are out on the streets day and night, as if they had nothing better to do. And they have two types of faces: some have perpetual concern in their eyes, whereas the others have a special sleepiness and limpness. The streets run on and on until they finally turn into alleys two or three feet wide, though even then they have names. Nothing grand or melodious, but names just the same. Real streets there are called Bonaparte, Goethe, Byron, Dante, Mozart and Cicero. But I can't tell you anything about them, I can tell you only about the alleys. These have barber shops where tramps get their hair cut for free – the student barbers practise on them. You run a great risk of someone building "stairs" on the back of your head, but tramps are brave and – all is flux! – life goes on and it grows out and a week later you're a human being again. Besides the barber shops there are also lots of little shops where you can pawn things and drink up the proceeds. Once a man pawned his wooden leg and then hopped from bar to bar. There are charitable institutions, of course, that look after the homeless and the drunks. For instance, there's the Low-Cost Sanitorium for Alcoholics, that's what's written on the sign; there are children's shelters named after David Copperfield. And of course there's the Salvation Army – God grant it health! – you can always tell them by their drum; the slang for them is Sally. You go straight from the pavement into a big room where people are singing in unison:

How wondrously the world is made:
Water enough for all to drink,
Bread enough for all to eat.
Glory be to God, I sing.
More wondrous still in heaven.

There are places where you first have to sing in the chorus and then you can go wash up and have a bowl of soup, and also get your mattress. It's called the four S's: salvation, soap, soup and sleep. There are others, three S's, where there's only salvation, soap and sleep. There are some even more involved combinations, too, but it's not worth going into. It's already late and I should be going.'

She stood up, watching thoughtfully as I stubbed out my cigarette and walked to the door.

'If you like, we could go to the country next Sunday,' she said, standing between me and the door. 'That is, if the weather's good.'

'If I like,' I repeated. 'Of course I'd like. Would you?'

'Isn't it obvious that I do?' she said, and she smiled. I'm the only one she smiles at like that, I thought, and I kissed her hand and left.

It was summer, the honeysuckle was blooming and fragrant, and we were sitting over the water, above the bay, where hundreds of sailboats were rocking on the waves, racing far away and turning back again. I looked in her face for the expression that had been there that first time I saw her in Kalyagin's study, but I didn't find it – although it had been there, it had come out so markedly then, more in that scene she staged at her first introduction to me, and that meant it would come back again. But each time we met she pushed that old self further and further away. Her look, her voice, her movements – everything was reborn before my very eyes, and it was no longer a smile but a very youthful, quiet, almost child-like laughter, carefree and lucid, that now accompanied our long conversations. And I kept looking into her face and thinking that it had been stern, that its foundation was hard, but now it was being transformed into something quite different.

'It seems to me,' she said, first sipping coffee from her cup, then cutting up a pear with a knife and offering me a small piece on a fork, 'that there is no Chicago. Wait, let me explain it to you. There's a strange, scary, immense city that you know a lot about but that neither you nor I will ever see. Instead, it's as if you and I both were already living there.'

'You might not see it, but I certainly will.'

She didn't respond.

'I'm going there very soon, there's nothing keeping me here.'

She looked at me in a strange way.

'Why don't you take me with you?' she asked completely seriously.

I laughed. 'What would you do there?'

She turned to the large dark blue mirror that hung on the wall over our table and examined herself closely.

'No, I don't have a horse face,' she said sadly. 'Have you noticed how as women get older they look more and more like either fishes or birds or trained dogs? I think in twenty years or so I'll fall into the third category.'

'You've got a long way to go to old age,' I said, laughing.

But she didn't laugh. 'Tell me, Evgenii Petrovich,' she said, having suddenly decided something. 'If I had a horse face, would you take me with you?'

She was speaking in all seriousness, but I didn't know what to say to her; I was suddenly gripped by a silence that I couldn't break.

In the evening we sat on the dunes, listened to the sea, lay back and looked at the sky.

'No,' she said suddenly, 'I don't believe that the stars are so far away, millions of light-years. That simply doesn't mean anything. One day they'll discover that they're much closer, and everything that used to seem infinite and immense will suddenly turn out to be quite small and much closer.'

'In Paris,' I said, 'there are sometimes street fairs: a circus, freaks, acrobats, fortune tellers, archery. Once an enterprising, self-taught astronomer set himself up in a booth. The barker (there are still barkers over there, like a hundred years ago) shouted into the megaphone, 'Hey, you, come on in, see the stars for fifty centimes. You live like moles, you don't believe in God, you have no feeling for beauty – at least take a look at the stars!'

Now she laughed merrily, raised herself up on one elbow, saw that I was sitting up and looking at her, cautiously pushed me down on my back, laughing all the while, lifted my face to the sky, grabbed me by the chin and repeated, 'At least take a look at the stars!'

I put one arm under my head and started to look at the sky. 'Those barkers are amazing people – failed public speakers or something.' I started talking again, lying on my back. 'Now, in Chicago . . .'

'Yes, in Chicago . . . What in Chicago?'

'There failed orators give entire speeches. One of them will get up on an empty soap box at some intersection where there's scraggly broom growing instead of a tree and start to give a speech, for instance, about effective poverty — how to extort the maximum amount of money from passers-by with the least expenditure of energy. It's a science in itself! Or here's another one — about finding free entertainment.'

'There's no such thing!'

'You can take a walk in the park and admire nature, you can listen to a wind orchestra in the city parks for free, you can find an old newspaper and read it from cover to cover, old newspapers being more interesting than new ones. You can compose a ballad and sing it on some corner and people will listen to it all the way through — that's just how people are. You can attend free courses to learn which mushrooms are poisonous and which aren't, and when the Australian aborigines devised a calendar. You can stop in at a museum once in a while, and if there aren't any, then you can go to the harbour and admire the outdoor tattooing. You can also spend an hour or two standing underneath a staircase admiring women's legs. But the best entertainment of all is the health questionnaire.'

'What kind of questionnaire?'

'Health statistics. It's great fun. They give you a questionnaire and you write whatever you want. How many times a week do you have dinner? How many times do you sleep outside? How many times a week do you wash – and a box where you put an x: with hot water, with cold water. Do you accept charity? When was the last time you worked? Once a man wrote, "Forty-two years ago". Why aren't you working? "I don't want to!" Some write, "I'd want to work but only on condition that I do what I like, because otherwise life isn't worth living." And the young lady asks you, "So what would you like to do?" And the man says, "I'd like to raise flags." "What kind of flags?" "National flags that they raise on holidays. I'm a specialist in flag-raising and I'm very partial to holidays. And I'm not going to do anything else."'

There was a long silence. With her, it never weighed heavily.

'You know, Evgenii Petrovich,' she said after a while, 'with you I feel quite different. No one would ever recognise me now. It's because you are not in the least bit afraid of me. You can't imagine the happiness when someone isn't afraid of you.'

'Why are people afraid of you?'

'Ask them. I think I already told you that my husband left me because I had no sense of humour whatsoever, that I was too conniving and cold for him. He even admitted that sometimes – not that he was afraid of me but that he was wary. Can you understand that?'

'I think so.'

She put out her hand and placed it on mine. We were both lying on the sand looking up.

'He also said once, "You live as if a tiny clockwork system were running inside you day and night, and you know I like to listen to the nightingales once in a while, and make mistakes." I thought a great deal about that.'

She took her hand away from mine and turned on her side, resting her head on her elbow, looking at me, and smoothing the fine sand with her deeply tanned hand. The sand was like snow under her fingers.

'I feel I want to listen to you and to tell you about myself,' she said after a pause. 'And I treasure every minute with you. Before I met you I always thought I knew myself well, my limits, so to speak. Everyone has their limits after all, don't you agree?'

'Yes.'

'But I suddenly realised that I don't know myself at all. And instead of feeling lost, mixed up, insecure, I feel happy. And I feel like telling you about that.'

Again, we were silent for a long time, each thinking our own thoughts, and she moved closer to me, soundlessly, and put her head on my arm, by my elbow, and was still. Then she asked, 'Is it too heavy?'

I answered, 'No, keep it that way.'

Later we went to the car and raced back to town along a broad, moonlit highway. She loved driving fast, and was calm and confident about it. Pulling up in front of my door, she held out her hand. My eyes met hers.

'You can be very beautiful sometimes,' I said, 'and good. When you want to.'

'I always want to . . . now,' she replied.

The car drove off, I went inside.

Summer was coming to an end. Everything that bloomed in the parks and squares had long since flowered and burned up in the sun. The city smelled of gas and dust. Every city has its own smell. Paris smells of petrol, tar and face-powder; Berlin, when I was younger, smelled of petrol, cigar and dog; New York smells of petrol, dust and soup, especially on hot days and hot nights, when the heat

can only be broken by a sudden thunder-
storm or a hurricane from Labrador or the
Caribbean. Time was starting to pass more
and more quickly and a fresh wind was
blowing in from the ocean, as Lev Lvovich
Kalyagin learnt from reading the newspapers.

We saw each other almost every day now. I
would go upstairs to visit Ludmila Lvovna
and have dinner with her. To the whirring of
the fan we listened to Bach and Mozart on the
radio, or talked. Sometimes we took a walk
or a drive somewhere. We already had our
favourite spots in Central Park. When we
crossed on the diagonals and came out at the
other end, music was playing and couples
were dancing around in a circle at the open-
air restaurant. Here, where no one knew us
and we knew no one, we often sat until late in
the night.

One evening when the weather was especially close and it seemed that the humid
September day would never end, she
suggested we drive down to the sea, to the
very edge of the city, and there board a boat
that went to an island – a twenty-minute trip
altogether, and we could make it two, even
three times, until night fell and there was
some respite. I remember we reached the edge

of the city, the tip, very quickly. The sun was beginning to set, the street lights were being turned on. Three ferries were docked, ready to sail, and we boarded one of them and immediately were struck by the carefree feeling you have when you're sailing without knowing where or when you'll be back: a rare feeling to which you can almost never afford to succumb.

'Maybe we should ask where we're going anyway?' I said when we had sat down in the wicker chairs and the boat, having sounded its horn and let out a cloud of black smoke, began moving away from shore.

'It doesn't matter. It's too late now.'

We sat at the bow and could not see the city we were leaving behind. Before us was the sea, and a hot, windless, orange-grey evening; to the right, beyond the black hulks of the factories, the sun was setting and the bridges, smokestacks and buildings at first dissolved in the incandescent smoke-tinged air; and then, when the sun had set, all this seemed to arrange itself in a row on the horizon, against the background of the sunset, like a menacing black army gradually disappearing from view, merging with the darkening sky. It was quickly growing dark. Gulls hid, vanished and flew out overhead once again. We could hear the waves slapping around us, the engines running in the depth of the ship. Our chairs had been moved; we were sitting side by side, she slightly forward of me, leaning into the woven chairback, looking ahead and thinking about something, and I was looking at her, at her hair, at the contours of her head and neck, now so familiar and somehow oddly close to me. Suddenly she said:

'You know, we're not going the right way at all!'

'And just where were we thinking of going?'

'I don't know. Only we're going somewhere entirely different. We're turning around. Interesting, will we go back or will they take us somewhere and leave us?'

At that moment the ticket-taker came up. We bought two tickets and found out that the ship was making a big circuit, circling the island, stopping twice and returning at around midnight. 'How nice,' she said. 'How nice.'

'You know, in Chicago there are children,' I said, watching the shores slip farther and farther away from us and the air darken, 'who don't steal, don't beg and don't sell their bodies. They play cards, day in and day out.'

She turned to look at me.

'They set themselves up in a vacant area where a building has been torn down, on a pile of rubble, put a collapsed, legless couch there or bring an old mattress from some nearby dump, and gamble around the clock for four, sometimes five days. They have skinny faces and tightly pursed lips. Sometimes they actually have children. Rarely, though. And the old men just *sit there*. By a chain link fence, under a tree, near statues and, naturally, in specially designated places. They just sit there. For this a small fee is exacted, but sometimes not even that. The old people just sit. They have a few distractions and that's it. That's how the days, months and years go by. And they go on sitting there. Their only pleasure is in choosing where to sit. Here, if you want. There, if you want. And choosing where to sleep: in the night shelters there are sleeping cells on two levels and they're all identical so far as I can tell, but they choose all the same. The cell locks from the inside. They can hook the latch from the inside, you understand, not from the outside! They can also choose what to eat: kidney beans, peas, green beans, sweetcorn. No one is forcing them, they each have their own food-tin. There's no official ration but a ration that is chosen, individually eaten, protected by that latch. A bed and a food-tin each.'

'Was he ever there himself?' she asked, narrowing her eyes slightly.

'Who?'

'You know, your friend, the horsey one.'

'N-no. He wasn't. He's just interested. He's lived there a long time, and he's always been intrigued by oddities. It's too late for him to change now. Not him.'

'Are there really people like that?'

'Not only that, he says that it reverberates somehow with a deep chord in his soul.'

'I understand.'

'Sometimes he expresses himself oddly. You have to put the chords of his soul in quotes.'

'I understand that, too.'

The boat sailed on and on, night was falling, blue-black, lit up, all with a hint of salt and smoke.

'I'd like to take a look at his letters . . . '

I didn't meet her eyes, I started looking to the right; the water was sparkling and playing there.

She and I both immediately forgot the names of the places where we were going. They didn't mean anything to us. When it got completely dark and the shores disappeared, she turned towards me and said, 'Tell me now, at last, about yourself, about your life. You evidently aren't going to take me with you to Chicago. All right, let's leave it at that. Have you always been on your own?'

'No,' I replied. 'Not always. But for the last ten years I have.'

'And before that?'

The moment I had thought of so many times in recent weeks had come, and with an effort I spoke the words.

'Before that I was married. I was married for fifteen years. I was happy.'

Ludmila Lvovna sat up very tense and straight in her chair. Even in the darkness I could see the anxiety in her face, as the contours seemed to sharpen. Her eyes grew larger.

'And I thought, Evgenii Petrovich, that you had never had relations with a woman.'

I was silent and thought how this trip to nowhere might turn out to be the last time we spent together.

'Why don't you say something,' she continued. 'You were married, you were happy. Is that really all, a happy man?'

The last two words sounded devoid of all meaning. I couldn't utter a single word in response. My old thoughts, difficult thoughts about myself, returned with new force – thoughts about my inability to forget and be reconciled, to change inside, to become strong, thoughts about the terrible crack that had lived in me for millions of years.

'You are, in fact, a happy man,' she said in a new voice (or was that her former, old voice, with which she had spoken at one time and then stopped), 'the first happy man I've ever met. There has been grief, of course, how could there not? It happens to everyone. But then, you see, you lived as you wanted, you reconciled yourself, you forgot. You flit around the world as free as a bird, you don't love anyone, you don't want to love anyone. You don't suffer, you don't want to suffer. And I, I must confess, thought that you were someone special, solitary in a special way, the kind of person who is always looking for something, who doesn't know where to go, or who to trust . . . You fooled me!' There was jeering in her voice.

But I wasn't sure whether she was joking or serious. I answered barely audibly, 'If you were to give me a bomb I'd . . . '

She laughed, 'You? A bomb? You'd give it right back, very politely, frightened out of your wits. Better if someone gave me a bomb. I know who I'd throw it at.'

'Who?'

'You, of course.'

It was night all around. We were sailing on the open sea; it was the ocean, a mysterious night-time passage. Below, on the lower deck, an orchestra was playing softly and an invisible black woman sang the blues in a low voice that was no longer young. At these latitudes it had the same resonance as our gypsy songs.

She was sitting facing me now, her elbows on the arms of my chair, her face close to mine.

'Marry me, Evgenii Petrovich,' she said, as if she couldn't stop herself, as if she were being swept along. 'Marry me for all time. Can't you see how good I feel with you? And you know why? Because I become someone else when I'm with you, someone new, someone real, someone I've probably never been with anyone else. I'm *funny*, especially right now, this very moment, don't say no, because now I realise what that means. Utterly defenceless and still funny! I become someone different because you're the kind of person I've never met before in my life. What kind of person are you? I'll tell you: in the first place, you're not afraid of anyone, including me. In the second place, you're very happy. Yes, yes, don't interrupt me – happy and free and honest. You don't mind me discussing you as if I were talking about some third person? I could use the third person: he's honest and vigorous and . . . '

This suddenly became unbearable.

'Ludmila Lvovna,' I said. 'Be quiet. I have no idea how you've managed to deceive yourself to such an extent. I'm weak, good-for-nothing, I'm racked with indecision, I lack what everyone else has – the ability to die inside and come back to life. I don't like life or people, and I'm afraid of them like most people are, probably even more than most people. I'm not free, I haven't really enjoyed anything for a long time, and I'm not honest because I didn't tell you anything about myself for so long, and now, when I do, it's so difficult.'

'Tell me just one thing,' she asked quickly, interrupting me. 'Can I go on loving you?'

In that instant she saw my face and took my hand.

'Keep quiet, don't answer. I understand. Forgive me for tormenting you.'

I took her hand and kissed it. I was so grateful to her for withdrawing her question. What would I have answered her?

A few minutes later she had calmed down

completely. I went below to bring her some iced coffee. She drank it and played with the straw. We stood amid the lights of some dock, then once again departed into the black night. And at moments it smelled as salty as the real ocean, so that it seemed as if we were sailing to Portugal.

But by midnight we were back.

'Still,' she said, holding on to me as we walked down the ramp, 'how nice it was. How nice! And neither of us has the slightest idea where we were. It's just as if the whole world belonged to me, everything in it but you.'

But something in her face had changed, I noticed, as had her movements and her voice. Once again that hard, angular, stern foundation showed through, a solid shape emerged that became her face. It was as if she didn't feel well. I didn't see her smile again that night.

A week later, I was in Chicago.

III

First, an unfamiliar train station, the feeling that I'd arrived at the very centre of something whereas in fact it was anything but the centre, the centre was far away, perhaps to the right and perhaps to the left – we had arrived somewhere off, to one side. But that's hard to believe: in a strange city it always seems as though the centre is wherever you happen to be right at that moment.

Then, the charm of posters, a blue, pink, green world, an imitation of reality that is too precise to be true. The better the imitation, the less you believe in it, the less you recognise the world in which you were born and are going to die, where so much is left unfinished, unspoken, unappreciated. The more unreal the depiction, the more it affects us. The spaces of a train station. A white day breaks through the windows. A crowd. A child eats ice cream. The dog wants some too, but doesn't get any. Someone's suitcases all piled up. It's a shame, dog, but there's nothing you can do. The taxi rank on the street. I have the address written down right here. The street has a fine name, but of course not Cicero or Byron. They say there are three theories as to why Byron was in such a hurry to get to Greece that time, but I think there was a fourth reason. There's only one theory as to why I'm here right now. (And not only am I not Byron, I'm not even the dark horse; I come only fifth, or eleventh, or three hundred and eighty-sixth.)

I tell the driver the address. I'd like to hear how a man with a nape like that expresses himself, that is, which words he uses and where he keeps them. We are driving fast, and the centre of the city, which for me had been the train station, goes with me: this corner, where people are buying papers from a newsboy; this intersection, where we've stopped for a red light. I imagine a life where all the lights are green, like emeralds, sprinkling life all the way to the horizon. And there, beyond the horizon, a turn, and again – the pointsman's wife stands with a green flag, just like in a children's cartoon. And there's no reason for it ever to end, unless she catches a bad chill or some fatal tumour is suddenly discovered – and it has to be a fatal one.

It's very noisy, very crowded, but no noisier or more crowded than other cities. I've seen many of them in my time, big and little, and I've appreciated and loved them. At one time both of us had loved them, but then they started collapsing around us one after another. After that we started to be a little afraid of them.

So I had arrived. I still can't make out anything but the notes in my hands, which are passing into the driver's. Then the change pours from his into mine and I climb out with my two suitcases. A woman opens the door. I've never seen her before. She was once married to my cousin, he died a long time ago, now she's married to someone else. Six grown children: two of her own, two from her second husband by his first marriage, two of their own. She leads me through a series of strange rooms: a parrot in one, an aquarium in another, a cat in yet another. She offers me eggs and cold roast beef and takes me upstairs to the neighbours, where a room has been let for me.

'There are other tenants, but they're quiet,' she said. 'Nice people, educated.'

'I'm quiet too,' I tell her, and I see that she believes me and smiles. I'm trying to memorise her features so that I'll recognise her on the stairs or on the street, but for some reason I can't.

The room turns out to be better than I'd thought: light, warm, clean. The hallway smells of coffee. Next door a record-player is playing softly. This is definitely a place in which I could live, and then I'd see, maybe I'd move on . . . The tea kettle would sing songs to me in the evenings, I would read books, write letters, go to the cinema and meet the people who lived to the left and right of me. To the left I'd find someone who loved order, a harmonious life, discipline, when B follows from A and leads to C. To the right I'd find someone who loved his nightmares, whims and anarchy. And I would vacillate between them and go to work and love in equal measure both my order and my nightmares. And the big Mediterranean lake would lie before me (this was when I took walks on the shore), and I would tell myself over and over that I had actually made an effort, I had found within myself the strength to resist, the will to pull myself out of the state I've been in for so many years.

How many years? Ten years had passed since she'd died, but nothing had gone, nothing was forgotten. Alya's clear face had watched me leave with excruciating sorrow;

Ludmila Lvovna threw her grandfather's antique clock on the floor. But what did I care who Homer talked with in heaven? Once, on a train, many years ago, between Freiburg and Zurich, I heard a conversation in the corridor at night: an old colonel was telling an engineer from Schaffhausen about how his wounds wouldn't heal. Ten years had passed since that global madness had ended (the first, believe me, there will be others!), and his wounds still ached.

I was standing nearby and listening (in those days absolutely everything fascinated me). 'Yes, young man,' the colonel put his hand on my head, and for a whole minute, petrified, I tried to decide whether or not to take offence from my position as a fifteen-year-old passenger. 'It won't heal up, the old stinker. It aches and aches, and I'll end up with gangrene.'

For years now nothing in the world has mattered to me, but people don't like that. They stop noticing you, and the mirrors stop reflecting you, and the echo stops answering you. I'd like to get better, but I just can't. I can't shake off that black pestilence, I can't be resurrected. Millions of years have passed since the day she died. I fly somewhere I don't know, I spin, I live in places it seems I never went to. And I am a mirror which no longer reflects anything.

She had everything I hold dear in this solar system, all the rest was Neptune and Pluto. When she was by my side, I had no desire to look through interesting picture books. Music and the starry sky both reached me as if refracted through her. In her the whole world revealed its lovable face, and all the rest was Neptune and Pluto.

From the window of my room I could see . . . here follows a detailed list that riveted me to that window, to that city, from the skyscraper to the blue trousers hung on the line. In the room there was the following furniture . . . another list; in this way I'll have objects all around me, and I'll be in the middle of them. If only I could retreat from this quasi-life, back to my free, marvellous, immortal, just, shared life.

If only I could return to the world healthy, still strong, take up various interesting hobbies, marry and have children. My wife would be quiet and meek; at night she'd shade the light of the lamp so that it wouldn't bother me, she'd economise on the house and look after sick kittens. Or maybe she'd be clever and would make accurate, intelligent remarks, use expensive perfume, raise one eyebrow and narrow her eyes. Then the old colonel moaned on his berth from the other side of the partition, at the same time as I was calculating the speed of the new arctic ice-breakers – the final fascination of my brief adolescence. I heard him grinding his teeth: 'Damn knee!'

No, I don't have what I need to heal the loss, to reconcile myself to my nightmares, to adapt myself cleverly to my own catastrophe. A Personal Catastrophe. I don't care about the world's, I'm not interested in them any more. I don't even know whether or not there have been any, these past few years. But it wasn't always like that: in the cellar of a certain building, in a certain city, at the other end of the world, where once we were buried, I lay on top of her in order to cover her. 'I am a king, I am a slave, I am a worm, I am God!' Together we shook as did the cellar and the entire building, until it collapsed on us. That was one of our most joyous and most terrifying nights of love.

Her whisper. Her moans, Her sob. Her cry – and one more. At that very second, a deafening thunderclap and the six-storey building began to rock. The sixth and fifth stories flew up into the air. The fourth and third crumbled to earth and the last two shuddered for a long while, sprinkling us with sand and plaster from the ceiling. Her eyes were still closed and two tears emerged from under her eyelids, two tears of final bliss.

Then the cellar ceiling started to give way, but not the walls. Deafened by the thunder all around, I tasted plaster in my mouth, going down my throat. Pieces of plaster were falling around and upon me. My left elbow was broken. She was motionless beneath me. She was silent. A thin stream of blood began to trickle slowly out of her round ear, under my chin. I lost consciousness.

Then came the stretchers. My love. My life. Mutilated. Silenced.

The doctors said there was nothing to be done. So did the jeweller: it's always been there and it always will be. 'Nothing to be done' – what a familiar phrase. That's what the doctors said, only not to the old colonel but to me, when she was lying whiter than a pillowcase and only her eyes seemed alive. They were alive one more day after that. Then I had to close them.

I don't know who to write to first: Alya or Ludmila. Alya asked me to write about myself and how I was getting on, which would be a lot easier to do. Ludmila asked me to write about Druzhin, and that's very hard. She must have guessed that there never was any Druzhin, that I dreamed him up, that I was going without knowing where I was heading. To nowhere, to see no one. That can happen: a person will be going somewhere where he doesn't know anyone, and there will turn out to be friends all around. With me it was the opposite. It all started one fine day when someone said to me, 'Make an effort, Evgenii Petrovich. You can't go on living like this. It's not right. You've got to . . . ' Maybe it was Barrister N., that troubled soul? I wonder what's become of him?

I unpacked my bags, washed and went out. The front door slapped me on the shoulder; it had been a long time since anyone had slapped me on the shoulder. Although Kalyagin had two evenings before. He'd said, 'I never expected such peculiar behaviour from you. You've put me in a tragic position. I'm too old to allow myself the luxury of changing secretaries.' He went into his bedroom without shaking my hand. I walked to the door, trying not to go faster. There was no one there, no one in the whole house, in the whole world. I went down the empty stairs, walked down the empty street to the bus.

And now once again I was in a wasteland: my room was empty, the street was completely empty, and this city was empty as well.

The crowds, however, went back and forth, the space was filled with lights, the trees rustled and bent over my head. Far, far away tugboats moaned and bellowed, cars leapt out from underground and dashed back in again, the thick grey sky swirled overhead. None of it quite resembled the descriptions in that old book I'd come across once on a certain bench, on a certain Left Bank boulevard not far from the Pont Sully, where I sat waiting for the barber shop to open. I remember there were pictures and a map of the city. It lay there forgotten by someone, as if it had been waiting for me. And I'd thought, good, I agree, dear little book, I agree with you, I'll live again and see whether something comes of all this, after all. Even the dead are resurrected so why shouldn't I, as I'm alive? Only for that I had to do something, I had to make a decision, get moving, adapt, I had to invent cities, people, stories, my own life, pin in, walk in step, try to resemble other people. And it had to happen quickly, otherwise I'd turn into a vegetable.

I'll definitely write to Alya. She would have slept on my shoulder, lying in my arms, whereas I would have slept on Ludmila's shoulder – that's plain as day to everyone. I'll write to her, too. But, you know, I'm not going to write to anyone. I'd do better to spend my evenings walking the streets and searching for Druzhin – he has to be somewhere after all! I've got so used to the idea of him that maybe I actually will find him in the end. I can see him clearly before me: thoughtful, a little sad, a white spot on his forehead, a thick mane of reddish hair. We would have something to say to one another, something to discuss. If I don't find him then I'll move on. It makes no difference to me where I live. And I like new impressions, they ease the pain, and doesn't everybody want that? Especially when there's a fear – good people – that you yourself might soon become Neptune or Pluto.

The Comb

The bus marked 'Schliemann Square
—Great Fountains' moved off from the
statue. It was overcrowded, but I found a
seat. I sat down by an open window, stuffed
my small canvas duffel bag under the seat,
tossed my hat on the shelf. It was a noisy,
dusty evening, hazy from the heat of the day.
Crowds were walking through the streets,
going from stuffy, hot offices and workrooms
to stuffy, hot, city apartments, but I was
going out of town, as far as I could from
Schliemann Square, to Great Fountains.

These three days off hadn't just fallen into
my lap, I'd earned them. More than four
hundred people worked at the large agency
where I'd been employed for two years in the
modest position of junior accounts clerk,
starting from the people no one ever saw and
ending with the man wielding the broom,
whom everyone always saw, since he spent
entire days chasing papers and various kinds

of rubbish out from under our tables and chairs and into a broad red dustpan. Work time there was calculated by a special, complicated, poorly understood method. For weeks they would seem to be cheating us, then suddenly they would come out with a bonus. I hadn't had a day of holiday all year and suddenly: 'You have Tuesday the fourth, Wednesday the fifth, and Thursday the sixth, off.' This was the decision of the huge machine that issued us our salaries and our bonuses, that calculated who had the right to be sick and for how long and who should get time off when. This machine looked like the mausoleums which used to be built in cemeteries for four generations of a family.

Before I had started at the job, they broke through the ceiling to the next floor for this machine and added bracing under the floor. The employees simply deferred to it: it never made a mistake. Out of it came my time off, out of it came my bonuses, out of it came a dismissal for one young lady with golden hair and jangling bracelets because she was always late.

But the machine couldn't have new ideas. And once, while I was looking down at it from the balcony that ran around the big hall where we all worked, a strange thought occurred to me: a way to increase work time by one twenty-fourth a day, that is, a way of doing something which the people I never saw would like.

This idea was the consequence of an idle game of my imagination, a game that bore neither cupidity nor a desire to curry favour. I couldn't have cared less about those ideals pursued by the inventors of the prison peephole or the time-clocks that record how long an employee takes for lunch. It simply occurred to me that if work were to start an hour earlier every day, then that could, so to speak, increase production, without any perceptible harm. On Monday, say, the day would start at nine, on Tuesday at eight, on Wednesday at seven. A week later it would be starting at two in the morning, but since the entire city would have shifted over to this kind of accelerated life, it wouldn't matter. At the end of the year each individual would have gained about two weeks of life, which wasn't bad. As a consequence, satisfaction would be accorded not only to the exploiter but also to the exploited. After working for twenty-five years, the individual would be rewarded, so to speak, with an extra year of life.

The concepts 'day' and 'night' seem utterly outmoded to me. Now, when shops, restaurants, cinemas and hospitals are open at night, when one-fifth of the inhabitants of large cities work at night, it would be very simple to shift over to new tracks. The old concepts about how you should sleep at night and work in the day made sense in the days when it was light in the day and dark at night, when it was noisy in the day and quiet at night. Why must we live as our ancestors did? Wouldn't it make more sense to shift over to continuous activity? And wouldn't it make more sense to start building *down* in parallel with building *up*, in order to save space, assuming that lighting, air conditioning, heating and, of course, perfect ventilation, could replace light and air?

Such a law might follow: when a twelve-storey building is built, twelve floors plus, then twelve floors minus must be built as well, into the earth, where neon light, warm air, cold air, sea air would be supplied continuously, imperceptibly, noiselessly. For ten or fifteen years or so it might not be altogether comfortable, until people adjusted to it, but then after that! When people met they could add a plus or minus sign to their name: 'Petrov+', 'Sidorov−'. This means that if you were Ivanov−, then you couldn't have anything to do with Petrov+, you could never become friends with him, but it would be fine to be with Sidorov—. So once again, you've gained time.

My idea was running in my head for several weeks, like a well-oiled motor. I thought, instead of political speeches, prophecies, lengthy conversations over tea, long heart-to-hearts under a lamp, or leisurely strolls, we should give one another our final decisions of a public-moral or individual-psychological nature. For instance: 'Do good. It's often not at all profitable to do evil.'

'If you take something, return it. But don't give anything up to anyone.'

'Respect the healthy. Avoid the infirm.'

'Forget the elderly. They won't be around long.'

I remember, about a week ago, inspired by this idea, I called Didi and said I'd been missing her and would like to come over. This made her very happy – I heard her bracelets jangle into the receiver, and that very night I went over. She took a complicated dish which she'd probably slaved over for hours out of the oven, and it had puffed up, browned, spread out, and smelled of cheese. We sat down. Her girlfriend, with whom she shared the apartment, was playing the mandolin for us, self-taught. They had a whole shelf of teach-yourself books, and the girlfriend peered at the book as she played. I saw that Didi, too, peered at a book she was holding in her left hand as she stirred something in a saucepan.

'Why were you always late for work? There, you see? Now they've fired you,' I said rather dryly.

She looked around sadly. Her hair was so magnificent that I felt like pulling out the comb that held it and burying my face in it.

'Wait for the bus. Wait for the subway. The crowds. I couldn't make it,' she said.

'You should have got up earlier. The time will come when there will be plenty of room for everyone and no one will be crowded.'

'The Bomb?' she asked timidly.

'Not the Bomb, a double life,' I said. 'Someday I'll explain it all to you. Nothing terrible. I could tell you right now, actually: there will be just as much above ground as below, as much in the day as at night. And that will make for more time and space.'

The mandolin strummed very softly. I felt good, peaceful, even rather happy with them. 'Take your comb out,' I said.

The girlfriend immediately stood up. She left the room, taking her mandolin and her instruction manual with her, and a minute later music began again beyond the wall, starting from that same interrupted note. Exactly as if we were in Japan.

None the less, she did not take out her comb. At a distance her hair smelled to me like a mix of lily of the valley and roasted chestnuts, the kind they sell sometimes on street corners when autumn comes, and there was something autumnal in her burnished hair, too. It was during these moments that I had the idea of taking a trip with her out of town. Since I'd entered this enormous city where she and I lived I'd never left it. It was summer now, sultry, long, but shouldn't there be flowers somewhere, and leaves, and air, burnished as her hair?

'Let's go away somewhere,' I said quietly.

'Where?' she asked, again with a sadness that implied there was nowhere to go.

But nothing ever came of this because a week later she found a job and our lives never coincided — as if she were a plus and I were a minus. Or vice-versa.

The bus sped straight down the road. Hours passed. Outside the opened window passed houses, people, cars, signs, shops. I thought about Great Fountains, I thought about my three days, about the machine that had given them to me. It's never wrong, the senior accounts clerk told me, and that was right-true as well as right-fair.

I thought the sun had set, but a few minutes later it glimmered again on the other side of the road, though not for long. The lights were already on. Dusk fell slowly. Occasionally we made a stop, people got off, others got on. A small square flashed by with a large, low, grey bush in the middle around which children were running. The railway passed by us, and overhead was the highway, where cars rushed headlong towards us in an unbroken chain, directly over the trains below, reminding me in a way of my dreams of life in the future.

Possibly others have already had ideas, lots of them, about how to reorganise humanity. Every century – no, every quarter-century – some new improvement takes a sharp turn and new horizons open up. So it was with the eight-hour workday. Stop. Turn. Up ahead new ideals reveal themselves: free hospital-isation, old age pensions. That, of course, is the least of it. Another turn, another ideal: insured burials, free dental care. Now we are anxious to lengthen time, to extend space. I am coming to the conclusion that it's time for me to put all these thoughts down on paper, to send them somewhere and apply for a patent. Yes. Apply for a patent. New perspectives are opening up. Dozens, scores, millions of cities, reconstructed, reconceptualised. The days reordered, rationalised. Special machines to calculate everything the way it should be: who lives where, who lives how, who is what, who lives when. Divisions: family, work, recreation. Subdivisions: art, childrearing, means of transport... A place for everyone, even those who love solitude. Let them live!

'Solitude is no crime. There are people who long for it. Don't get in their way.'

'Strange as it seems, lepers have a right to live, too.'

Don't run these two slogans together; leave them separate, maybe even insert another in between: 'Leave your neighbour alone. He doesn't want your concern.'

I have to be prepared for assault on two sides. Any thought, even such ancient and now utterly meaningless thoughts as 'There is a God' and 'There is no God', are always under threat of assault on two sides: progressive humanity and the reactionaries. Especially a new thought. Progressive humanity – which has been embodied for nearly seventy years by the government which controls exactly half the globe and to whose throne ascended Kuzma the Second, nephew of Sidor the Great – progressive humanity is going to be at pains to lay a trap for me not so much from the standpoint of accomplishing my spatial tasks as from that of accomplishing the tasks they entail: those two weeks a year which, like a bonus, will fall to the working class (and all humanity), progressive humanity will immediately try to pocket, demanding that they be divided up among choral singing, atomic calculations, study of Sidor the Great's biography, and parades. Whereas the reactionaries, naturally, will rebuke me for holidays, fasts, the Gregorian calendar, the Julian calendar, reckoning time from the day of the appearance of the Star of Bethlehem and the earthquake in the Near East in the first century of our era.

But understand me, understand! I am by no means promising you an easy solution to all the world's problems. On the contrary, I'm drawing you into great difficulties: architects (above all!), stationmasters, doctors, engineers, writers, coal miners, tailors, housewives – everyone faces enormous difficulties . . . but then after! After, say, a hundred years or maybe two – what a relief! Until everything is all mixed up again in the crowd and the bustle, until some new genius appears with new ideas for reordering space and time.

A new genius. That sounds as if I considered myself a genius. That's not true at all, though. I'm a modest man: my ideal would be a job as a senior accounts clerk, maybe a junior book-keeper, marriage – and why not to Didi? What happiness it would be to be with her, to be with her always, and the main thing – to be loved by her. 'Do you love me?' I'd ask her every day, all day long. And she would answer each time, all her life, 'Yes, I love you.'

It was nearly dark when we finally stopped, pulled in under thick trees and parked.

'Great Fountains,' someone said behind me. We walked past a caged dog with which I locked eyes for a moment. I pulled my canvas duffel bag out from under my seat, put on my hat, and suddenly the anticipation of joy descended upon me. Not asking anyone anything, I got off the bus, walked out from under the trees on to a broad square, and stopped at an ice-cream vendor's stand. I listened closely, trying to work out which direction I should go – but I couldn't hear the babbling of water, although I remembered very well that fountains are supposed to babble.

Before me was a square. Streetlamps burned all around. The wide, utterly bare place was surrounded by an even ring of small trees, beyond which rose buildings, tall, stone, with lights on in most of the windows. There must have been a traffic jam in a side street because I could hear the howl of car horns from there. When it stopped I listened again, but there was no sound of babbling. Directly in front of me was a huge, dry, cement fountain pool, about sixty metres in diameter. It was filled with people.

'The fountains?' I asked the ice-cream vendor.

'Not working,' he said.

I walked over to the pool. I had the impression that I was still in the middle of a large city, that in fact I hadn't gone any-where. The purple and azure signs beyond the trees burned like the windows in the buildings, on floor after floor, like offices where evening cleaning was going on. It smelled of the same dust and cigars, and if it weren't for the gold-embroidered letters 'G.F.' on the ice-cream vendor's cap, I could have imagined I was somewhere not far from home – on the road to the tobacco stand, say, for I had to cross a boring square in order to get there.

A dull rumble of voices hung over the dry pool. It was full of people sitting, standing and lying. By the light of the streetlamps you could make out faces – young and old, in strange clothes. You could hear individual voices, voices whispering, singing, saying things; as if on that stifling summer night all these people had come out of their houses and somehow by accident, surprising even themselves, had stopped on the square, in this enormous basin – or better, on this enormous cement raft about to sail away into the expanses of the night. It's hard to say who was here, it would have been easier to name who wasn't. At first glance, there were several hundred people, a few cats, a few dogs, about a dozen children, and a large cage with a parrot that had to be taken out to breathe the night air, too.

A small group of people was standing in a circle in the middle of the pool and was getting ready to sing something. A fiddle and banjo lay at their feet Turkish fashion, but it seemed as if these people were about to unfurl the sails on the raft and cast off, with everyone now gathered here after a shipwreck, me included. I sat on the edge where someone moved over to make room for me.

There were old men who had brought

along folding chairs and chess boards; old ladies who had spread newspapers out under their seats and clutched fat purses against their stomachs; young girls lying in the arms of young boys and boys lying in the arms of young girls, children crawling over them, cats playing on the knees of a pregnant beauty; two tramps offering each other swigs from a flask; a lively, barely audible conversation between two people wearing sandals and Mexican belts; a bald man talking to himself; a red-lipped woman with impudent, bulging eyes, resting her arms on two young men, flashing her teeth at a third; and then a pale, middle-aged gentleman with a flushed, broad-cheeked face sitting with his back to her.

There was a bunch of housewives, fat, strong, all with the same face, in low-cut cotton print dresses, knee-length, sleeveless; over them hovered the odour of kitchen fumes. Young girls with boys' haircuts, wearing trousers, others with hair loose to the waist, a sixteen-year-old mother dozing over a child's pushchair; a few girl delinquents playing some wild game, collapsing on to their neighbours, toppling them from the edge of the pool, choking with silent laughter; formally dressed, in prim hats, girl twins with their Mama and Papa; huge blacks in vivid silk neckerchiefs and jackets over naked torsos; Spaniards with guitars; an effeminate cherub with an old, wise face; fat mothers' boys holding ice-cream cones in each fist; cripples with blank faces, ranging in colour from pale green to soot black; two freckled brothers in identical Scottish caps; some others too, apparently expecting something, having come here to the obviously long-dry fountains to breathe this night, to watch the moon rise slowly in the black-red sky; and there it was, instead of playing in the streams of the fountain, playing on the faces of this strange, sleepless crowd. Someone struck the strings, an African- or South American-sounding song played, some people joined in, especially among those lying in each other's arms. So the cement pool was filled with song, and all it lacked was the fragrant air of summer, the swaying trees and the hushed nightingales.

We sat there until about three in the morning, dozed and sang and dozed again. It was cooler than in those stuffy houses; freer, easier, and something reminded me of the tall spray and the resilient sparkle of the water. It smelled of dust. The ice-cream vendor was still standing at his post, but the buses were gone – the last one had sounded its horn and vanished around the corner. Like everyone else, I dozed and sang, and then I put my duffel bag under my head, perched on the pool's edge and fell sound asleep. And certain whispers and the quiet music all around shifted into my dream, and in my dream someone kept asking me about something, some three-syllable word that sounded like a question, a short, persistent question for which I had no answer.

When I awoke, the pool was nearly empty; there were no more than a dozen people still asleep in it. A stifling new day was beginning, and the sun was already burning, although it wasn't yet eight o'clock. I went to find some breakfast. Streets filled with morning city life ran in all directions. People were hurrying on their way, the newsman was opening up his stand, the shoe-shine man was roosting on his stools, coffee-houses were opening up, there was the smell of freshly baked rolls. I drank coffee and ate eggs, and it all reminded me of my intersection, where I lived, as if after a five-hour bus race I had wound up in the place where I'd started.

But that's not what I'd wanted at all! The machine that had given me three days off hadn't done it in order to . . . And suddenly I saw a long row of yellow-green buses, the sun blazing in their windows, their doors wide open. On the first was written, 'Blue Shore,' on the second, 'Green Shore,' on the third – some other shore.

'They're all going to the lake, more or less,' a man said to a woman as he seated her. 'Only this one, you know, skirts the city gardens, and that one runs along by the river, so what do you think, will that be quicker?'

From out of nowhere people started streaming in, the driver switched on the motor, and I, repeating to myself, 'blue shore, green shore, blue, green, pink gardens,' jumped on too, shoved my bag under the seat, tossed my hat on the shelf and sat down by an opened window. We howled past the empty pool, turned into a tight street, into another rather broader, into a third, and there I lost count. Hundreds of people were streaming in all directions it seemed, a wall of people, the enormous city rumbled all around. Whether it was the same one I lived in and had hoped to break away from yesterday, or another, contiguous and similar, or yet a third – I don't know. We roll-ed through it now without stopping, and it seemed there would be no end to it.

I thought back to the previous evening. There had been at least two people for every square metre in the dry pool. So you see, if my idea were used then there'd be half as many because there would be, say, only Pluses relaxing in the square after a sultry summer day, before falling asleep until morning and, in the morning, going back to work. During this time the Minuses would have wiped their eyes, gone under the taps, gulped down some coffee after jumping up with the alarm, scurried off to their factories, plants, offices, schools. Yes, there would be half as many people in the dry fountain, on this cement raft. I must jot down my plan, commit it, finally, to paper. Only in what form? That would take some thinking. And there was no better time than the present: the bus was now rolling down the highway, buildings flashed by now and then, the passengers dozed, the road spread out endlessly, to the edge, to the very horizon. And there, as I believed, awaiting me, beyond the horizon now, were blue, green shores.

If I were to write something on the order of a novel, then at this point people would be saying that I'd borrowed from the great utopians of our century. Not the idea, but the device itself, and perhaps even the manner of its exposition. But generally speaking, the predictions of all these geniuses have not been borne out, and we, in our one thousand nine hundred and fifty-eighth year, have not advanced all that far from our grandfathers' times. And then, after all, I intend to apply for a patent, this being a serious business bearing no resemblance to a utopia. If I have borrowed anything from the geniuses of the first half of our age, well then, they too borrowed without a twinge of conscience what they could from others who had lived earlier, especially our great-great-great grandfathers, so it works out that I'm taking back what belongs to me.

But no! Let's set the novel aside. It's better and simpler – and somehow more serious – to write a report and then submit it to the senior accounts clerk. (After all, I don't manage to exchange a word with even the junior bookkeeper more than twice a year!) Ask him to pass my memo up, and up, and up, and up . . . But there's no need to ask: the most important people are bound to take an interest in my idea. And they can develop it without me; I'm modest and entertain no fantasies of becoming chairman of any Special Space-Time Commission. Specialists, university departments, academics – they'll develop the idea. After yesterday evening, I'm convinced that all this has to be written down. Otherwise, before long there are going to be four people for every square metre on a moonlit, starry night in the municipal garden!

Despite the speed of the bus, despite the open windows, it was getting hotter and hotter. We were racing along now in the sultry, trembling air of a summer's day, the sun burned, the canvas shades were lowered. and I began to doze to the monotonous, silky sound of wheels in the turbid and dusty light. 'Leave your neighbour alone,' I thought. 'He doesn't need you at all.' That's another slogan. These slogans will lend my report a certain philosophical air. 'Do neither good nor bad to your neighbour; just forget all about him.' And little by little I started to doze in a sudden mood of sweet certainty that the emerald gardens and azure shores were coming closer and closer and could not escape me.

I woke up with a jolt. The bus had stopped and people were filing out; I got up as well. A second later I came to: this wasn't that first bus but a second one, I told myself; this is the second day of my trip, the middle of the second day. I jumped down from the step to the ground and looked around. Whether this was Green Shore or Blue, I didn't ask. By a small lake, on a flat shore, stood an enormous brick-glass factory which shuddered with clanging and rumbling. The gates of the main building were wide open, and there in the dark depths a foundry glimmered, reminding me somehow of the terrible red sun that hung over my head. Around the lake, as far as the eye could see, stood red-hot cars in cramped rows, all identical and of an indeterminate colour.

I stretched out alongside one of them in a kind of stupor, trying to tuck myself away in its narrow shadow, on the pebbles and cigarette butts. The black smoke that obscured half the sky came from the same direction as we had but did not end either over the lake or beyond it. There on the other shore was a twin of the nearby factory, also brick-glass, enormous, alive somehow: even from here you could tell that it was full of people, loud noises, the mechanical might of droning and shuddering. Past it, off to one side, stood a gigantic power station, completely transparent, similar in its intricate pattern to the skeletal Eiffel Tower.

I breathed in the hot air saturated with car exhaust. Despite the shadow, the side of the car I was lying alongside, which I tried not to touch, was red-hot; there was no breeze coming from the lake, and I was starting to feel sick from the petrol fumes that filled my mouth and nose, from the smell of scorching tyres, metal, oil. Where am I? How many towns have I passed through, towns that ran together in a blur? Where is the horizon I was promised? Where am I? What kind of lake is this, surrounded by droning factories, where's the grass, where's the forest, where's the field? Where do these streets go? To more houses, stores, signs, buses, other cars? And will people come here to swim as night falls, so that I can go into the water with them? But the water seemed lead-black, and metallic, like everything around here, and about thirty steps away from me was a signpost: No Swimming.

Two people were walking towards me now: one was wearing a service cap and the other, naked to the waist, was wiping his forehead and neck with a handkerchief and evidently looking for his car. They stepped over my hat, and I jumped up and shouted after them, louder than I should have, 'How do I get out of here?' I wanted to ask, Where's everybody else? But at the last second I thought the question would sound foolish.

'Turn right and the third turn will take you to the highway,' said the one in the service-cap slowly, having stopped and looked around at me.

'I'm on foot.'

'On foot?' The other one stopped too, and they both looked at me.

'When does the bus go?' I asked again, too loudly.

'The bus goes tomorrow morning,' said the first, and they walked on, farther and farther away from me. The half-naked one finally found his car, started it up, drove out and vanished in the dust. The first, in the service cap, walked back.

'Listen,' I said, quieter now. 'I'm in the wrong place. I was going to the lake. That is, I thought that this lake, well, you know how lakes can be . . . I went through four towns, four at the very least, there may have been five. I thought . . . I have a day and a half. Couldn't you tell me . . . '

'Ask at Information,' he said. 'You're not supposed to lie down here.' And he walked away.

I followed him. 'You understand,' I said, still trying to make him listen. 'I do have a sense of humour, and yesterday I had a terrific laugh when Great Falls, that is, I mean Fountains, played a trick on me.' (Did I really laugh? I have absolutely no memory of laughing!) 'But today it's too much, it's not funny any more. I'm angry, and most of all I'm angry with myself, and if you'd only listen . . . '

'Ask at Information, they'll tell you there.' he repeated, and I saw his face. It expressed nothing. Not even distaste. It simply lacked all expression, like a piece of paper or a china saucer.

My watch said a quarter to five. I was hungry, I was walking down a road between the walls of a factory that stretched to infinity. Then began the two-storey houses, where evidently the workers and employees from the nearby factories lived: porch–window, window–porch, and so on, to infinity, on an utterly deserted street, without a single tree, without a bench, without a puddle, without passers-by, without children. I walked for an hour and a half until I had passed through it all and seen nothing, apart from windows–porches. Then it came to a stop and I found myself, clearly, on the main street, because on the right and left were one petrol station after another. Then a square, large glass stores, three churches, a library, a school, a hotel. I walked in.

'Do you have a room?'

A room was found. I washed, changed my shirt, went downstairs, had dinner, but knew no peace. I was overwhelmed by exhaustion, by the heat and by a feeling of distress, like when your insides are in an uproar and you'd like to be in an uproar yourself, but you don't have the strength; you long to lie down, but as soon as you do the uproar inside you becomes even more powerful, and nothing you do will quiet it, unless sleep comes and crushes you completely, with your private poundings, all those pulses that beat inside you like steelworks, at an incredible depth that bears no relation whatsoever to your own manifest dimensions.

I awoke in the middle of the night and heard once again that same sound which last night – in my half-sleep when I was lying on the bottom of the cement pool – gave me no rest. I could hear a brief, persistent question, perhaps a single word with the stress on the second syllable, or three words, each one syllable long. Perhaps it wasn't a word at all but simply something striking triplets, or drops dropping – one soft, one loud, one soft, over and over, brief strokes – but no, there was some kind of word in that sound.

In the morning I went down to the restaurant where, despite the early hour, it already smelled of soup, like all cheap restaurants. I was served by the fat proprietress, who was wearing slippers on her bare feet and a clean apron. She had clean, calm hands and a motionless, once sweet face. I suddenly decided to tell her everything, so that she would tell me what to do. She listened to my story and sighed heavily.

'You came to the wrong place? But why didn't you ask? And it's been so hot! I always say it's better to take your holiday when it's not so hot, otherwise you just torture yourself. On days like this it's only nice on the Gulf.'

'What Gulf?'

'On the Gulf, on the sea. At the shore. At least – even if it is scorching – at least there's a breeze once in a while.'

'Is it far?'

'An hour and a half. No, sorry, more. Are you in a car?'

'No, I came by bus and then on foot.'

She looked at me with disbelief, and I added faintheartedly, 'That is, I walked here from the bus stop, assuming that there'd be buses and bus stops somewhere in town.' She was mollified. There was even a certain sympathy in her eyes.

'And you realise, time is passing.' I couldn't

hold back any longer. 'And I'm still trying to get somewhere, it's just stupid, and even if I did have a sense of humour, and I do, then all this might seem very funny. Just dreadfully funny, ha ha ha!'

She displayed a row of teeth – that's how she smiled – and then went to the other tables, but already all I could think about was the Gulf.

'There's a train,' she said, returning with the bill. 'You'll make it. It will take you right to the Gulf, it's a passenger train, a good one. It leaves in about two hours. You'll have a swim there, lie in the sun. Fine sand, glorious swimming. And a very broad beach, half a kilometre. The Gulf!'

I looked at her with gratitude. In that instant, with all the heart I could muster, I wished her prosperity, for her children, her grandchildren, prosperity in this hotel, in this restaurant, the smell of which pursued me all the way to the station.

My duffel bag – under the seat; my hat – on the shelf. The train cars went from station to station, small, hot, rumbling; the passengers changed, people flitted by, but I was happy, or rather, nearly happy, because regret over the time lost descended upon me like a dark cloud; it was hot, exactly like the day before.

If I tried hard I could imagine it was the day before, when I was lying in the narrow shadow of the strange car next to the sinister lake, and then that trek, and even before that the dry reservoir, and I lost count of the buses and towns, and I was no longer completely certain how long I'd been traipsing through those towns in those buses.

Once again the white-hot sky was in the window, and the sun – fortunately, on the opposite side – was baking, burning, shimmering. I was trying not to move, since with the slightest movement I was drenched in sweat. I looked out of the window and there, in an odd, chance order flashed tall buildings, smaller buildings, railway tracks in between, a piece of road, a tree jammed between two churches, a factory, a petrol station, another building, the trajectory of a street full of traffic, a street that seemed to be deserted, the criss-crossing of cables over everything, a station, a plane like a silver ant crawling across the sky, an elevated road running at an angle to our train, a bridge consisting of four bridges plaited between the highway and the streets – and so it went not for two hours, or three, but almost a whole four, when the train suddenly stopped, went a little bit further, and came to a final stop. I looked through the window, beyond the roofs, the chimneys, the church spires and crosses and the water towers, and I got a glimpse of the Gulf in the haze of the intense heat. It flashed for an instant before an oncoming train entering the station blocked it out. But I already knew it existed.

How is all this going to look in the future? That interests me, to be perfectly honest, much more than how it looked in the past. The past I can't change. The past is good (as we all know) – twenty, thirty years back *everything* was good, anyone can tell you that. On this, I think, both the progressive-thinking (as they are usually called), like that great mind Kuzma the Second, and any retrograde who believes in the evil eye, will concur. So I'm not interested in the past. But I can play a role in rebuilding the future, and although I feel no burning personal ambition, I have to admit that the thought comforts me in my – let's be blunt – grey life, in my utterly unremarkable fate. 'Who is that man?' someone will ask, and they'll tell him, that's the man who gained an average of one twenty-fourth of a life for each person and who doubled space. I absolutely must think everything completely through before I write my report, to say nothing of the novel. Sometimes I find it strange that all this hasn't occurred to anyone else. After all, there are people thinking (and people of the most diverse inclinations) about how to arrange the fate of mankind.

I moved with the dense crowd towards the Gulf. The restaurants were full, people were dining under colourful umbrellas, drinking iced drinks; music rumbled from a loud-speaker, interrupted by adverts. I have nothing against advertising, but I don't understand how people can like it more than music. Still after all, there are people who listen to music only reluctantly, relaxing at the adverts.

We started down a long tunnel, where it was cool, where people on holiday, or maybe on tour, lined the walls, enjoying the coolness, and a few people from our crowd stayed there, assuring us, 'It's better here.' But I didn't. The tunnel led us from one bend to another, until finally a light appeared in the distance, that same terrible, irrevocable sun flashed and the Gulf opened up, a watery expanse receding into the distance, into the haze, and I knew that I was going to look out at it until my eyes hurt, anything not to turn back onto the path I'd already travelled, to the six, seven, maybe even more towns I'd left behind.

Yes, everything was marvellous on that

scorching, sandy shore: in long rows to the left and right, their façades facing the Gulf, rose white skyscrapers which evidently occupied dozens of kilometres on the broad, gently sloping shore. We all took off our shoes and walked barefoot across the fine, burning sand, carefully skirting the prostrate bodies, carefully placing our feet so as not to step on anyone, stepping over strange feet, arms, sometimes even heads. The advertising howled, interrupted by the music; sometimes more adverts howled right underfoot, from radios brought along by the swimmers. People were settling down wherever they could find an unoccupied piece of beach, and I too quickly settled in among the bodies, hesitating for a second, trying to figure out if I was going to bump into anyone when I lay down. But someone politely shifted a little, or rather, flopped over on to his other side, and I moved, drawing my shoulders and belly in so as to take up less space. Around me I heard people breathing, conversations, snoring, children crying; for a while I didn't move, so as not to disturb anyone, then I threw off my trousers and shirt, and, dressed in my shorts, stretched out blissfully on my stomach, rested my head on my arms and was still. A helicopter flew over low, and its shadow brushed me for a moment. I moved a can, an empty bottle, a crumpled, half sun-faded newspaper someone had dropped on me away from my face and closed my eyes. It seemed to me that through the thousands of sounds – the drone of helicopters, the shrieks of swimmers, the howl of the radio, the lifeguards' whistles – I could hear the splash of waves. This was the imagination of a completely happy man – the Gulf was silent and immutable.

I must have dropped off. I came to and cautiously untangled myself from the arms and legs of my benumbed, dozing neighbours and, once again paying attention to where I placed my feet, walked to the water's edge and stood in line to swim. Here there was perfect discipline. The Gulf was filled with swimmers as far as the eye could see, and there were long lines of them waiting at the very edge of the shore for their turn, for when there would be room for them in the water. The sun was still burning, I felt like throwing myself, hands clasped, into the blue, absolutely flat, soundless wave, but there was nowhere to throw myself, it was all full, impossible even to squeeze in. People were standing shoulder to shoulder, holding children, diving cautiously, taking turns, obeying the lifeguards' orders. 'Taking turns,' I said to myself. 'This confirms my theory. It's interesting, what great mind thought up this idea of "taking turns"?'

Finally it was my turn. I went in. The water was warm, but still refreshing. I went in up to my chest; the people were fewer, and I swam off. Ahead was the far shore of the Gulf, or so I surmised, and I kept watching it, and the haze of the heat in which it disguised itself as an ocean. 'Away, away, together, one day.' I began speaking in verse suddenly from the fullness of my sense of lightness and hope. 'In the end it's not so far, there are probably steamboats, very clean, very white, smelling as if they'd been rubbed down with cologne, and you and I will take a steamboat like that, cast off, sail away. And there won't be anyone there, or almost anyone, or only people like you and me, and you and I will stay there not two days or three but as long as the machine allows, the good, intelligent machine. If we wait two years or so, we'll have that shared happiness – and how marvellous it will be: a forest, a field, a pond, birds and flowers.'

That hazy shore seemed to me like the promised land. I loved it, I dreamed of it, and it seemed to me this love was beginning to change into another, into something I had never been able to feel inside, something I had dreamed of experiencing so many times but still somehow hadn't been able to, because something was missing.

I turned back and half closed my eyes; ahead I saw everything I'd so wanted to leave behind. There, behind those glass-marble, pink-white skyscrapers approaching the water, lay poisoned lakes, dry fountains, towns stretched out over a grid, one emerging from another and leading into the next. There were stifling dusty nights, sultry dusty days, junior bookkeepers and senior accounts clerks, and you, you, whom I lectured so drily and harshly, with such dispassion, for being late to work, citing as an example myself, who have never been late for anything! With half-closed eyes I swam and swam, and it seemed to me that at any moment tears would start flowing from my eyes, mixing with the salt-water of the Gulf, tears of compassion and love, and tenderness, and eternity. Feeling the bottom with my feet, I stood up and walked, still remembering that behind me across the Gulf, in the blue smoke, lay another world I had been alone in for a brief while, far from everyone – my world of silence, of our shared solitude, and of joy, also shared.

But up ahead it was the same shore, the crowd covering so much of it that if anyone asked me what colour the sand was I wouldn't know what to answer; the sun swimming in the sky, already slightly slanted to one side of the buildings, and the lines of people waiting in perfect discipline for the moment a place came free in the water. And over it all that noise, when you can't hear your own voice.

I pushed through to get out of the water, pushed through to get to my spot, dried off as best I could, brushing my neighbours' faces with my towel and constantly begging their pardon. I couldn't find room to lie down on the cramped beach any more, so, gathering up my things, I went to eat. I waited patiently in line, ate a lot, drank a bottle of beer, wandered down the burning pavement under artificial palms, listened to the loudspeaker forecasting a clear evening and relatively cool night, and sat down on a stone bench. Evening was starting to fall. The sun went behind the skyscrapers.

'It would be nice to stay here till morning,' said a woman's voice; two people were sitting next to me, a man and a woman.

'But we've already reserved a room,' he objected, 'and made a deposit.'

'He said it was going to be a clear evening and a cool night.'

'Yes, he did.'

'And we can swim again when no one's here, and sleep on the sand.'

'If everyone thought like that, no one would ever leave, and it would be just as crowded.'

'That couldn't be. Eventually almost all of them will leave. In any case, half.'

I smiled but held my tongue. She had said it: half. I'll soon give them what they want. They don't know it yet.

'It'll be rough sleeping,' said the man, and he yawned.

'It's the air which makes you do that,' said the woman. 'Yes, maybe you're right.' They were both silent.

'You know what –' he suddenly reached out dreamily – 'let's go.'

'Let's,' she agreed. And they stood up and walked away, leaving me to my thoughts.

They flowed, those thoughts, and in an unconscious but close connection with them incoherent feelings were awakening inside me, all the time pursuing my thoughts, over-taking them, exactly as if they were weaving some kind of fabric combining two threads of different colours in one design; as if two shuttles were flying inside me, and if I weren't afraid of seeming old-fashioned I would have said that one was in my mind and the other in my heart, one was related to my idea and the other to Didi. Two threads weaving together, and then suddenly the first shuttle began to leave the second behind, getting far ahead, growing dim. It didn't seem so important, so significant, so decisive; whereas at that point the second was somehow managing to deck itself out in gold, rust, autumn colours. And amidst all this, suddenly that question, that three-syllable night sound that this time didn't seem to want to wait for the night, but amidst the noise, the shouts, the running, the crampedness, the ever-burning but now oblique sun, it rustled, flowed through, 'Where are you?' And then, about five seconds later, again, 'Where are you?' And again, after a silence within me, 'Where are you?'

And suddenly I realised that mankind needed nothing from me, that there was no reason to split space and give each person a time extension so that life could suddenly go on longer than it now did, so that the lines of swimmers could suddenly become half as long – that this still wouldn't fix anything. I realised that only one thing is necessary and important: the shore of the Gulf, in the rain, in the snow, in the burning heat, in storm and blizzard, where she and I together, with my one and only forever, are going to be, as much as possible, as much as the machine allows us, so that passing through the fields and forests like two guardian angels (she being mine and I hers), we can feel that only she can forgive me everything and I her, only she can protect me, and I her, from everything in the world, past and future. I realised that this walk which is going to happen – there can be no living otherwise – will be our betrothal, and wedding, which is and can be none of anyone else's business in the world. In those minutes despair and joy seemed to intertwine inside me into one unbearable lump, the shuttle flew in mad disarray, pounding loudly: 'Where are you? Where are you? Where are you?' The fabric was being woven, the very foundation of my life, and I was hearing and seeing her – as happens perhaps once or twice in a man's life.

When I came to after all this the sun was gone and the crowd at the shore had thinned. I walked along the shore, at the water's edge, where now you could pass without brushing anyone. I walked and walked. On the left of me skyscrapers stood in a solid, endless wall, sparkling now in the lights of advertisements; on the right, barely audibly, the green-blue Gulf vacillated. In the distance, where the shore took a turn, on the background of a darkened sky, a gigantic screen lit up and giants were already moving around on it, the show had begun. Now I was quiet inside – everything was silent, everything was calm, as if some kind of decision had been reached.

Before lying down on the still warm sand, I gazed into the distance for a long time: the crowd was still thinning out; someone was still splashing in the dark water; a few people a little way away from me were getting ready to eat, spreading a cloth for a picnic; the air became quieter, gulls flew by slowly, one more plane droned by overhead. I stretched out, not parallel but cross-wise, so that my face was to the horizon and my back to all that had been, in order to feel that this time I was lying on the edge of my former life, that right here, by this Gulf, it came to an end, and beyond it another began.

Night fell. The picnic was over. I began to doze off, my head on my duffel bag. Sleep approached so slowly, so cautiously, that it seemed as if I felt its approach with every moment, as if it were a spirit barely touching the earth, walking towards me. It seemed as though someone was placing a hand on my forehead and that the long tresses of her hair were streaming slowly and smoothly between my forehead and her palm. And then I fell asleep and must not have moved all night because when I opened my eyes in the morning I was still lying on my side, my arm stretched the length of my body.

I opened my eyes and didn't move: directly in front of me the dawn was breaking. A long, pale stripe stretched across the Gulf, and on the horizon, where yesterday the hazy smoke had wearied and tempted me, stood a huge, black city, the eighth or ninth, by my count, blocking the horizon in a concave semi-circle.

I lay immobile, gazing at the immense black silhouette of the city. The broken line of its roofs was precisely drawn on the pink dawn; the skyscrapers retreated in tiers. And I wasn't surprised that this hard, black vision arose from out of the water, or that it was lowered into the water through a narrow break in the early-morning clouds that luxuriated overhead and through which the sun was already reaching out to the water and land. What amazed me about that vision was its conjunction of horror and beauty, the death of something that had scarcely arisen in me, and the return of what had always been there, of something familiar, something I had lived with, something I had grown used to, something I had made my peace with, I think. It was growing now, setting its limits before me, its laws, and there could be no question of rebelling against it or arguing with it, or of conducting any kind of dialogue with it at all. The city stood, indisputable, like that law. And above it, behind it, the sun was rising, about to be transformed from a black silhouette into something translucent, into lace made from iron, concrete and stone, barring the way where I had thought there was a possibility of retreat – for an hour, a day, or forever.

The day was beginning, but that scorching air I'd been breathing the days before seemed to have dispersed, and a coolness was borne in from the Gulf. The couples and solitary people who had fallen asleep on the sand had not stirred, everything was quiet, life had not yet begun; only from somewhere, probably the nearest coffee-house, came the first broadcast of morning news. I stood up. For a minute I hesitated – take a swim? But I had no desire to go in the water. I put on my shoes, turned towards the shore, and without looking at either the Gulf or the sun shining in the heavenly glades, strode off towards the voice of the loudspeaker.

The next day I was sitting in an armchair, in a room, and she was on a stool beside me. I was telling her that all in all there was no point going anywhere, that fountains don't gush, there's no swimming in lakes, there's no room for anyone in the gulfs, but soon all this was going to change.

'The Pill?' she asked, raising her sad eyes to me.

'Not the Pill. I've already told you, but you're so scatter-brained and you never listen to anyone and you forget everything.'

Then I told her about my return trip, which was shorter than I'd expected, and how we had wound up back on Schliemann Square again.

'I dare say you don't know who Schliemann was?' I asked condescendingly, sensing my superiority over her, all the seriousness, all the practicality of my nature.

'No,' she said, but there was no notable regret in her voice.

'Schliemann discovered Troy,' I said, examining my cufflinks. 'That's why they erected a monument to him. Do you know what Troy is?' She shook her head. No. 'He made excavations, he excavated nine cities. The ninth was Troy. Vertically, you see, they lay on top of each other.'

She'd shaken her head, the comb had fallen out, and her hair spilled down.